Grace tried to gather her scattered thoughts. Jack's body felt lean and hard and disturbingly hot. When her hands fanned against his midriff, she could feel the heat of his skin through his shirt.

And knew she should put some space between them.

She tilted her head and looked up into his dark, compelling face, and their eyes met.

Jack's exclamation was harsh, but unmistakably passionate. And when his hands tightened on her arms, she felt all the bones in her legs turn to water.

"We—we have to go," she said, but her voice was thready and barely audible.

Jack nodded. "Yeah," he said hoarsely. But then he bent his head and covered her lips with his and she fairly melted against him. Which was so wrong. But just at that moment it felt so incredibly right.

Dear Reader,

Although it's been three years since my last Harlequin Presents book was published, I haven't been wasting my time! I've written a long book, which took a little longer than I had anticipated and is still a work in progress, and three Harlequin Presents romances. The first is *A Forbidden Temptation*, and I really hope you like it. It is set in the north of England on the wild Northumberland coast, which I believe is one of the most beautiful coastlines in the UK. I'd also like to take this opportunity to thank all my readers, some of whom created the Anne Mather Fan Club on Facebook. I love reading all the posts and I hope my new books will generate some more.

Thanks for everything.

Anne Mather

Anne Mather

—

A FORBIDDEN TEMPTATION

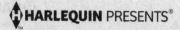

Recycling programs
for this product may
not exist in your area.

ISBN-13: 978-0-373-13893-7

A Forbidden Temptation

First North American Publication 2016

Copyright © 2016 by Anne Mather

Printed in U.S.A.

www.Harlequin.com

Anne Mather and her husband live in the north of England in a village bordering the county of Yorkshire. It's a beautiful area, and she can't imagine living anywhere else. She's been making up stories since she was in primary school and would say that writing is a huge part of her life. When people ask if writing is a lonely occupation, she usually says that she's so busy sorting out her characters' lives, she doesn't have time to feel lonely. Anne's written over 160 novels, and her books have appeared on both the *New York Times* and *USA TODAY* bestseller lists. She loves reading and walking and browsing in bookshops. And now that her son and daughter are grown, she takes great delight in her grandchildren. You can email her at mystic-am@msn.com.

Books by Anne Mather

Harlequin Presents

Innocent Virgin, Wild Surrender
His Forbidden Passion
The Brazilian Millionaire's Love-Child

Latin Lovers

Mendez's Mistress

Queens of Romance

Bedded for the Italian's Pleasure
The Pregnancy Affair

The Greek Tycoons

The Greek Tycoon's Pregnant Wife

For Love or Money

Stay Through the Night

Visit the Author Profile page at Harlequin.com for more titles.

I'd like to dedicate this book to my loyal readers, whose letters have given me so much pleasure.

CHAPTER ONE

THE PHONE WAS ringing as Jack walked into the house.

He was tempted not to answer it. He knew who it would be. It was at least three days since his sister-in-law had contacted him. Debra seldom ignored him for very long.

But she was—had been—Lisa's sister, and he supposed she was only looking out for him. The truth was, he didn't need looking out for, he thought resignedly. He was doing just fine on his own.

Dropping the bag containing the still-warm baguette he'd bought at the village bakery onto the granite counter, Jack hooked the kitchen phone from the wall.

'Connolly,' he said, hoping against hope that it might be a cold call. But those hopes were dashed when Debra Carrick came on the line.

'Why do you insist on turning off your mobile phone?' she greeted him irritably. 'I called you once yesterday and twice today, but you're never available.'

'And good morning to you, too,' Jack commented drily. 'And why do I need to carry a mobile phone every place I go? I doubt there's anything you need to tell me that can't wait.'

'How do you know that?' Debra sounded offended

now and he stifled a groan. 'In any case, what if you had an accident? Or if you fell off that stupid boat of yours? You'd wish you had some means of communication then.'

'If I fell off the boat, the phone wouldn't work in the water,' replied Jack mildly, and he heard Debra give an impatient snort.

'You've always got an answer, haven't you, Jack?' she demanded, her frustration evident. 'Anyway, when are you coming home? Your mother's worried about you.'

Jack acknowledged that the worrying part might be true. But both his mother and his father—and his siblings, come to that—knew not to ask those kinds of questions.

They'd accepted that he needed to move away from the family. And this house he'd found on the wild Northumbrian coast was exactly where he wanted to be.

'This is my home,' he said now, glancing round the large farmhouse kitchen with a certain amount of pride.

When he'd bought the house, it had been in a sorry state of repair. But after months of his living out of suitcases and cardboard boxes, the renovation—a lot of which he'd done himself—was now complete.

Lindisfarne House had emerged as a comfortable, but elegant, home. The ideal place to find refuge and decide what he was going to do with the rest of his life.

'You're not serious!' He'd almost forgotten what his answer had been until Debra spoke again. 'Jack, you're an architect! A successful architect at that. Just because you've inherited that money doesn't mean you have to spend all your time bumming around some godforsaken corner of England!'

'Rothburn is not a godforsaken corner of England,' protested Jack civilly. 'And certainly no more remote than Kilpheny itself.' He sighed. 'I needed to get away from Ireland, Debs. I thought you understood that.'

Debra sniffed. 'Well, I do, I suppose,' she conceded. 'I'm sure your grandmother's death was the last straw. But all your family's here. Your friends are here. We miss you, you know.'

'Yeah, I know.' Jack could feel his patience thinning nonetheless. 'Look, I gotta go, Debs.' He grimaced at the lie. 'There's someone at the door.'

With the phone hooked back onto the wall, Jack spread his hands on the cool granite for a moment, breathing deeply. It wasn't her fault, he told himself. Just because every time he heard her voice he found himself thinking about Lisa didn't make her a bad person.

For God's sake, he just wished she would get off his case.

'She's in love with you, you know.'

The light, half-amused tone broke into his bleak mood of introspection. He lifted his head to find Lisa seated on the end of the counter, examining her nails.

She was dressed in the same cropped pants and silk blouse she'd been wearing the last time he'd seen her. One high-heeled sandal dangled from her right foot.

Jack closed his eyes for a moment and straightened from his stooped position.

'You don't know that,' he said flatly, and Lisa lifted her head and met his brooding gaze.

'Oh, I do,' she insisted. 'Debs has been in love with you for years. Ever since I first brought you home to meet Daddy.'

Jack turned away and picked up the baguette he'd brought home from the bakery. Despite his conversation with Debra, it was still warm, and he switched on the coffee pot and took a dish of butter from the fridge.

Slicing himself a generous wedge of the baguette, he spread it thickly with butter. Then forced himself to eat it, even though he disliked having her watch him do so.

'Are you going back to Ireland?'

Lisa was persistent, and, although Jack despised himself for humouring her, he turned his head. She was still sitting on his counter, a pale ethereal figure that he knew from previous experience could disappear in an instant. But today, she seemed determined to torment him and he lifted his shoulders in a careless shrug.

'What's it to you?' he asked, lifting a mug from the drainer and pouring himself some coffee. Strong and black, the way he liked it. 'You don't like Northumberland, either?'

'I just want you to be happy,' Lisa said, spreading her fingers as he'd seen her do a hundred times after she'd applied a coat of varnish on her nails. 'That's why I'm here.'

'Really?'

Jack was sceptical. In his opinion, she was doing her best to make people think he was crazy. He was talking to a dead person, for God's sake. How insane was that?

A draught of air blew across his face and when next he looked, she was gone.

She left nothing behind. Not even the faint trace of the perfume she'd always worn. Nothing to prove he wasn't going out of his mind as he sometimes suspected he was.

In the beginning, Jack had dismissed Lisa's appearances as a mental aberration. Even so, he'd gone to see a doctor in Wicklow who, in turn, had sent him to a psychiatrist in Dublin.

The psychiatrist had been of the opinion that it was Jack's way of grieving. And as no one else saw Lisa, Jack had half believed he might be right.

But the visitations had continued, sometimes with days, at other times weeks, in between. Jack had become so inured to them that they didn't worry him any longer.

Besides, he'd never felt that Lisa wanted to hurt

him. On the contrary, she always appeared as quirky and capricious as she'd been in life.

Jack scowled and carried his coffee out of the kitchen and across a wide panelled hall into a sun-lit living room.

The room was large, high-ceilinged and furnished with dark oak and leather. Pale textured walls contrasted with the beams that arched above his head, long windows overlooking the coastline and the blue-grey waters of the North Sea.

There was a leather rocking chair set in the window embrasure and Jack seated himself in it and propped his booted feet on the sill. It was early yet, barely nine o'clock, and the day stretched ahead of him, silent and unstructured.

Which was also the way he liked it.

As he drank his coffee he pondered the prospect of taking the *Osprey* out for a sail. He knew from previous experience that manning the forty-two-foot ketch demanded all his energies. The North Sea, even at the end of May, didn't take any prisoners.

He frowned. He wasn't sure he wanted that kind of action. He might spend some time on the boat. There were one or two jobs requiring his attention. And he enjoyed exchanging the time of day with the fishermen who also used the small harbour.

Not that he really needed the company. Although he'd suffered in the aftermath of the accident that had killed his wife, he wasn't suicidal. Besides, it was nearly two years since Lisa had died, for heaven's sake. He should be over his grief by now.

And he was. Mostly. Except when Lisa herself turned up to torment him.

When had she first appeared? It must have been about a month after her funeral. Jack had been visiting her grave in the churchyard at Kilpheny when he'd realised that Lisa was standing beside him.

God, she'd certainly shaken him out of his apathy that day, he remembered ruefully. He'd half believed they must have buried some other young woman by mistake.

But no. Lisa had quickly disabused him of that notion. In any case, despite the fact that her little sports car had burst into flames on impact with the petrol tanker, dental records and DNA evidence found at the scene had proved conclusively that the remains they'd found were those of his wife.

The only thing that had survived the crash unscathed had been one of her designer sandals. Which, he assumed, was why Lisa only ever appeared wearing one sandal these days.

He used to ponder that anomaly. Why, if Lisa herself could appear apparently unscathed by the experience, couldn't she have been supplied with another sandal?

It wasn't important. After that first shocking encounter, Jack had learned not to question such prosaic irregularities with her. Lisa had her own agenda and she never deviated from it.

She enjoyed provoking him. Much as she'd done during the three short years of their marriage. Anything else was apparently beyond her remit.

He scowled, finishing his coffee in a single gulp and getting to his feet. He couldn't spend the rest of his life analysing what might have been. Or, as Debra had said, 'bumming around'.

Or talking to a ghost, he appended drily. Perhaps he ought to be wondering if he was losing his mind.

Eight hours later, he was feeling considerably less gloomy. He'd spent the morning doing some minor repairs to the ketch. And then, because it had been a beautiful afternoon, with only a mild wind flowing from the south-west, he'd taken the *Osprey* out on the water.

By the time he drove back to Lindisfarne House, he'd forgotten how introspective he'd been that morning. He had a bucket of fresh shellfish he'd bought from one of the fishermen and some fresh greens in the back of the Lexus. He was looking forward to making a lobster salad for his supper.

He was propped against the fridge, drinking an ice-cool can of beer, when he heard tyres crunching on his drive. Dammit, he thought, slamming the can down and heading for the front door. The last thing he needed tonight was company…

He scowled. He didn't get visitors. Not visitors who parked in his driveway, anyway. No one, except his immediate family, knew where he was living.

And they had strict orders not to give his address to anyone.

When the doorbell chimed, he knew he had to answer it.

'Why don't you open the door?'

Jack swung round abruptly to find Lisa perched on a half-moon console table.

'Say what?'

'Open the door,' she said again, and for the first time she looked almost animated.

'I'm going to,' he said, speaking in a low voice, hoping that whoever was outside wouldn't hear him. 'What's it to you? I'm the one who's going to have to entertain an uninvited guest.'

'Two uninvited guests,' amended Lisa, evidently implying that he had more than one visitor, and Jack's brows drew together.

'So who are they?'

'You'll find out,' she said lightly, her image fading even as her words were dying away.

Jack shook his head, not sure what he ought to make of that. Lisa rarely if ever appeared twice in one day. Did something about the visitor—*visitors*—disturb her? Perhaps he ought to be on his guard. He was alone in the house, after all.

Well, as good as.

Pushing such negative thoughts aside, he released the latch and opened the door.

A man was standing outside. A man he hadn't seen in God knew how long. He and Sean Nesbitt had grown up together. They'd even attended university together, sharing a flat in their final year.

They'd graduated from Trinity College, Dublin, and had been eager to gain advanced degrees, Jack in architecture and Sean in computer science. After leaving Trinity, however, they'd both gone their separate ways, only meeting occasionally when they'd been visiting their parents in Kilpheny.

Since Jack's marriage to Lisa, he'd virtually lost touch with the other man. And he had to say, Sean was the last person he'd expected to see here.

'You open for visitors?'

Sean was grinning at him and for the life of him Jack couldn't have turned him away.

'Hell, yes,' he said, taking the hand Sean held out and then stepping back automatically. 'But, my God, what are you doing here? And how the devil did you find me?'

Sean's grin widened. 'I'm a computer expert, remember?' he said smugly, glancing back at the silver Mercedes he'd parked on Jack's drive. 'But I'm not on my own. I've brought my girlfriend with me.' He pulled a wry face. 'Is it okay if we both come in?'

So... Jack lifted a thoughtful shoulder. Lisa had been right. He did have more than one visitor. But...

'Sure,' he said, not without some reluctance, casting a swift glance over his shoulder as he did so. But the table was unoccupied. Lisa had definitely gone.

'Great!'

It was only as Sean turned to go back to the car that Jack realised he hadn't changed since he got back from the marina. His cargo pants were smudged with paint and his black sweatshirt had seen better days.

Ah, well, they would have to take him as they found him, he thought resignedly. He hadn't been expecting visitors. And wasn't that the truth?

Sean had circled the car to open the passenger-side door to allow a young woman to get out. But she forestalled his efforts, sliding out of the car before he reached her door. From his position in the doorway, Jack could only see that she was tall and slim, and dressed in jeans and a white tee shirt.

Sean was only of average height and build and in her high-heeled boots she was almost as tall as he was. She also had a mass of curly red-gold hair, presently caught up in a ponytail.

She didn't immediately look his way and Jack wondered if she was as unenthusiastic about this visit as he was. But Sean was a friend and he couldn't disappoint him. Not as he appeared to have come quite some distance to see him.

Sean attempted to put an arm about the girl's waist to draw her forward, and Jack felt a momentary pang of envy. How long was it since he'd had a woman in his arms?

But to his surprise, the girl shrugged Sean off, striding towards the house with a determination that wasn't matched by the expression on her face.

Uh-oh, trouble in paradise, mused Jack wryly. He must be right. She hadn't wanted to come here.

Then he caught his breath. He felt suddenly as if he'd been stabbed in his solar plexus. His involuntary reaction stunned him, the surge of heat invading his lower body feeling like a fire in his gut.

His response was totally unexpected. Not to say inappropriate, as well. He didn't do lust, but that was what he was feeling at that moment. Dammit, she was Sean's girlfriend; he'd said so. And just because they'd apparently had a lovers' tiff didn't mean he had the right to pick up the slack.

But she was striking. High, rounded breasts, pointed nipples clearly outlined by the thin cotton of her tee. Her thighs were slim and shapely, and she had the kind of legs that seemed to go on for ever.

Thank God for his baggy cargo pants. He had the feeling he had more than his reaction to hide. He almost broke out in a sweat at the possibility that Sean might notice.

He couldn't believe this was why Lisa had been so keen for him to open the door. Yet, wasn't it just the kind of quirky thing she would do? She'd enjoyed baiting him in life and she still enjoyed baiting him now.

Of course, Sean's girlfriend was nothing like Lisa. Lisa had been petite, blonde, bubbly. And okay, yes, she'd been flirtatious. But judging by the look he was getting from this girl, she was anything but flirtatious. She was regarding him with cool—what? Indifference? *Contempt?* As if she'd guessed exactly what was going through his mind.

Right.

Stepping back, he made room for them to come into the house, and Sean quickly made the introductions.

'Grace Spencer, meet Jack Connolly,' he said cheerfully, and, despite the look from her amazingly green eyes, Jack was obliged to take the hand the girl reluctantly offered him.

'Hi,' he said, aware that her slim fingers were cool against his suddenly sweating palm.

'Hello.' Her voice was as cool as her expression. 'I hope you don't mind, but Sean asked me to come with him, to show him how to get here.'

'I— No. Of course not.'

Jack frowned. He detected a slight local accent. Did she come from this area? If so, how on earth had she met Sean?

Realising he'd been silent for too long, he said awkwardly, 'Do you know the area, Grace?'

'I was born here,' she began, but Sean didn't let her finish.

'Her parents own the village pub,' he said quickly. 'Grace left here when she went to university, and she's been living in London since then.'

Jack nodded. At least that explained the connection. The last he'd heard, Sean had been working in London, too.

'But I've left London now,' Grace inserted flatly,

giving Sean what Jack thought was a warning look. 'My mother's ill and I've decided to move back to Rothburn to be near her. Sean is still living in London. This is just a flying visit, isn't it, Sean?'

There was no mistaking the accusation in that question. Jack felt his eyes go wide, and his inhibitions about this visit increased. Whatever was going on here, he didn't want to be part of it. But they were evidently not the happy couple Sean was trying to convey.

'We'll see,' Sean said now. Then, squaring his shoulders, he forced a grin for Jack's benefit. 'I bet you were wondering how I found you out.'

'You could say that.'

'Well, when Grace's pa said an Irishman had bought this old place, I never dreamt it might be you,' Sean continued. 'It wasn't until they mentioned your name that I put two and two together. Small world, eh?'

'Isn't it?'

Jack inclined his head. He hadn't tried to hide his identity from the locals. But no one really knew him here; no one knew about Lisa.

He just hadn't expected Sean Nesbitt to turn up.

'So…' Jack tried to inject a note of interest into his voice now. 'Do you come up here every weekend to see Grace and her family?'

'Yes—'

'No!'

They both spoke at once, and Jack could see the sudden rush of colour that stained Grace's cheeks.

'I come as often as I can,' amended Sean, his pale blue eyes darkening with sudden anger. 'Come on, Grace, you know your parents are pleased to see me. Just because you're feeling neglected, that's no reason to embarrass Jack like this.'

CHAPTER TWO

GRACE WAS ANGRY.

She knew she shouldn't have let herself be persuaded to come here with Sean, but what could she do? Apart from the obvious misconceptions it created, she didn't like arguing with him in public. With Jack Connolly looking on, she felt hopelessly embarrassed. He was not the kind of man to be fooled by Sean's lies.

The trouble was her parents expected her to marry Sean, and they would certainly have suspected something was wrong if she'd refused to come with him. For now she had to accept the situation. But she refused to let Sean make a fool of her.

It had been so different in the beginning. When she'd first met Sean, she'd been fascinated by his easy charm. Okay, she'd been young, and naïve, but that was in the days when she'd taken everything he said as gospel; when just being around such a popular older student had given her a feeling of pride.

How wrong she had been.

Her first mistake had been bringing him to meet her parents. With Sean's promises of easy money, her father had been persuaded to mortgage the pub to help finance Sean's fledgling website.

Grace had tried to stop him. Even though she'd

believed she was going to marry Sean, she'd known the website was a huge gamble and her father knew little about websites or their uses.

But Tom Spencer hadn't listened to her. He'd thought he was investing in her future and she'd loved him for it. But even then she'd had some sleepless nights worrying about what would happen if the website failed.

And it had. Like so much else where Sean was concerned, the dream hadn't equalled the reality. Even now, her parents had no idea that Sean had lost their money. Which was why Grace had to do everything in her power to get it back.

Even if it meant lying about her relationship with Sean.

Her parents were still labouring under the illusion that Sean was only staying in London to advance his business. She knew they thought she should have stayed with him, but Grace had had enough. She'd stopped short of telling them about the scene that had finally ended their relationship. Until her mother had recovered her health, she couldn't lay that on them, as well.

She'd let them think that she had been homesick. When the sickness she had felt had been of a different order altogether.

But Sean knew their affair was over. And if she had her way, soon she'd never have to see him again.

But now, here they were, standing in Jack Connolly's doorway, and she for one would have liked to turn around and go home. It was obvious Connolly didn't want them here. And she couldn't exactly blame him. So why didn't Sean get the message and put an end to this embarrassing stand-off?

Unfortunately, their host seemed to realise his manners just as Grace was searching for the words to get them out of this.

'Please,' he said. 'Come in.' And he moved behind them to close the heavy door.

Grace was still wondering why Sean had wanted to come here, anyway. What was it he'd said: that Connolly had lost his wife in a car accident a couple of years ago and that this was his first opportunity to offer his condolences to the man? Grace had had to accept it when he'd strung that line to her father, but she'd have said Sean was the last person to offer sympathy to anyone. Unless there was something in it for him, she appended with the bitter knowledge of hindsight.

Or was she judging him too harshly?

And then she remembered another titbit he'd offered. Apparently Jack Connolly had inherited some money from his grandmother and that was how he'd been able to buy this place. Sean's take on it—or rather the one he'd offered her father—was that Jack had wanted to get away from the pain of familiar places. He'd moved to Northumberland to find a place to lick his wounds in peace.

Having met Jack now, Grace took that with a pinch of salt. Whatever he was doing in Northumberland, he didn't look like a man who had any wounds to lick. He seemed perfectly self-sufficient, and far too shrewd to need anyone's sympathy.

She hadn't forgotten the way he'd looked at her when he'd first seen her. It hadn't been the look of a man who was drowning in grief. On the contrary, if she and Sean had still been together, she would have considered it offensive.

Were all men untrustworthy? she wondered. She didn't think so, but she had no doubt that Jack Connolly wasn't to be trusted, either.

It annoyed her that he was also drop-dead gorgeous. Even the thick stubble of a couple of days' growth of beard on his chin couldn't detract from the stark male beauty of his face.

His skin was darkly tanned, as if he'd been spending time in a sunnier climate. But, according to her father, he'd been living here throughout all the renovations he'd made to the house.

Unruly dark hair tumbled over his forehead and brushed the neckline of his sweatshirt. Thin lips below hollowed cheekbones only added to his sensual appeal.

They crossed the hall and entered a well-lit living room. Whatever she thought of Connolly himself, there was no denying the man had taste. Pale walls, dark wood, much of it antique from the look of it. And a Persian carpet on the floor that fairly melted beneath her feet.

Grace headed for the windows. Despite the attractive appointments of the room, she was fascinated by the view. It was stunning. And familiar. It was still light outside, and she could see the rocky headland curving away, grassy cliffs beyond a low stone wall falling away to dunes.

The sea was calm at present, reflecting the reddening clouds that marked the sun's descent. Lights glinted in the cottages that spilled down the hillside to the harbour and the small marina, the distant cry of gulls a lonely mournful lament.

The outer door slammed and Jack Connolly strode into the room to join them.

'You'll have to forgive the way I look,' he said ruefully, flicking a hand at his paint-stained pants. 'I've been on the boat all day and I haven't had time to change.'

'A boat? You've got a boat?' Sean was enthusiastic. 'Hey, what's it like to be a millionaire?'

Grace, hearing Sean's words, felt her stomach sink within her. Oh, God, why hadn't she asked him how much Jack had inherited? Why had she simply assumed it would be a moderate sum?

What price now his condolences for Jack's wife and his grandmother? Jack's supposed grief had been forgotten. Sean had simply used it as an excuse to get her here.

Jack, to his credit, didn't call Sean on it. 'Let me offer you both a drink,' he said. His eyes shifted to Grace as she reluctantly turned from the window. 'What would you like?'

Well, not you, she thought childishly, disturbed in spite of herself by those heavy-lidded dark eyes. What was he really thinking? She wasn't sure she wanted to know.

'Got a beer?'

Sean didn't wait for her response, but Jack apparently had more respect.

'Um—just a soft drink for me, please,' she said, remembering she was starting a new job the following day. The last thing she needed was to have to face her boss with a fuzzy head.

'A soft drink?' Sean rolled his eyes at Jack. 'Can you believe this woman was brought up in a pub and she doesn't like beer?'

The twitch of Jack's lips could have meant anything. 'I won't be long,' he said and disappeared out of the door.

It was only as Grace heard the faint squeaking sound as Jack crossed the hall that she realised his feet had been bare.

She looked at Sean then, but he only raised his eyebrows in a defensive gesture.

'What? What?' He glanced away to survey the huge comfortable sofas and armchairs, the heavy bookshelves and inlaid cabinets with an envious eye. 'Some place, eh? I bet this furniture is worth a fortune. Aren't you glad you came?'

'Uh—no.'

Grace could hardly bear to look at him. She should have refused to come here. Sean was a pathological liar. She'd known that, but she'd also not wanted to cause an argument and endanger her mother's health.

'A millionaire's pad,' went on Sean, when she didn't elaborate. He turned his attention to a picture hanging on the wall behind him. 'Hey, this is a Turner! Can you believe that?'

Grace didn't want to talk about it. Whatever way you looked at it, she was here under false pretences, and she didn't like it. God knew, she didn't care about Jack Connolly or his money. He couldn't solve her problems.

Jack came back at that moment carrying two bottles of beer and a glass of cola.

'Please—sit,' he said, setting Grace's glass on a low polished coffee table where several expensive yachting magazines were strewn in elegant disarray.

Deliberately? Grace didn't think so. Despite the little she knew of the man, she didn't think Jack Connolly would care what other people thought of his home.

Jack put Grace's glass on the table and, to his relief, Grace seated herself on a plush velvet sofa beside the coffee table. And Sean, after accepting his beer from Jack, did the same.

'Hey, great place you've got here,' he said, waving his bottle around with a distinct lack of regard for the safety of its contents. 'Where'd you get all this stuff? It looks expensive.'

Jack propped his hips against a small bureau he'd picked up in an auction room and said, 'A lot of it was my gran's. The rest I bought and restored myself.'

'No way!'

Sean stared at him, and Jack could see the disbelief in the other man's gaze.

'Yes way,' he said and took a mouthful of his beer. 'It seemed a shame to get rid of it.'

Sean shook his head. 'Since when have you been a furniture restorer, man? You're an architect. You design houses, shopping centres, schools, that sort of thing.'

'Yeah, well—'

Jack didn't want to get into his reasons for doing what he'd done, but Sean wouldn't let it go.

'Oh, I get it,' he said. 'Now you've got private means, you don't need a job.'

Jack bit back the retort that sprang to his lips and said instead, 'Something like that.' He took another gulp from his bottle. 'Beer okay?'

'Oh, yeah. It's cold.' Sean nodded. 'Just the way I like it.'

Then he glanced suggestively at Grace. 'Well, beer, anyway.'

Grace cringed. Why couldn't Sean just drink his beer and stop being so crass? It was so embarrassing.

And, as if he'd sensed her discomfort, it was Jack who came to her rescue.

'So what are you doing these days?' he asked, addressing himself to the other man. 'Still inventing computer games for that Japanese company?'

'Well, no. As a matter of fact, I don't work for Sunyata any more. I've been doing some consulting until I can get my own website off the ground. We can't all have your advantages, can we, Jack?'

Jack blew out a breath. How the hell was he supposed to answer that? He just wished this uncomfortable interview were over.

Forcing a smile to his lips, he met Grace's unwilling gaze with a feeling of resignation. But he pressed on, anyway. 'How about you, Grace?' he asked.

'Grace has a law degree,' broke in Sean before she could say anything. There was pride in his voice, despite the lingering touch of animosity he'd revealed before. 'She used to work for the Crown Prosecution Service.'

'Really?' Jack was impressed.

'Not that there are jobs like that up here,' Sean went on bitterly. 'Grace has had to put her career on hold.'

Grace sighed. 'I'm very happy with the job I've got,' she averred shortly. 'Can we talk about something else?'

'But you, working for an estate agent!' Sean was scathing. 'You know you can do better than that.'

'Sean!'

Grace stared at him with warning eyes, and, as if realising he wasn't doing himself any favours, Sean grimaced.

'It's a living, I suppose,' he conceded. 'I may even try to find myself a job in Alnwick, too.'

Grace shook her head disbelievingly, but Sean's expression didn't change.

'Well, I could,' he insisted annoyingly. 'I might enjoy a change of scene.'

'I don't think so.'

Grace knew he was being deliberately provocative. Was it all for Jack Connolly's benefit? The last thing she wanted was for Sean to move up here.

But as if sensing what she was feeling, Sean reached out and took her hand.

'You know how I feel about you, don't you, baby?' he crooned, bestowing a lingering kiss on her knuckles. 'I know we're having a few problems right now, but once you're back in London...'

Grace gritted her teeth. 'I'm not going back to London, Sean.' She'd told him she wanted to stay near her parents, but he refused to believe it. She'd also made it clear that they could remain in touch—in the hope of recovering her parents' money, although he didn't need to know that—but any relationship between them was over. Did he think that by talking like this in front of Connolly he'd convince her to change her mind?

Meanwhile, Jack stifled a groan. If Sean and his girlfriend were having problems, he didn't want to hear about it.

And despite Sean's mournful expression, he didn't think Grace was too thrilled about it, either.

Or was that only wishful thinking?

And, if so, where had that come from?

Grace had succeeded in pulling her hand away now. For want of something else to do, she wrapped both hands round her glass and concentrated on the cola fizzing away inside.

She'd known Sean was selfish, but his behaviour was unforgivable. He was supposed to be sympathising with Jack, but he hadn't even mentioned his wife's death.

Taking a sip of her drink, she put her glass down and got to her feet.

'We should be going, Sean,' she said firmly.

Sean swallowed another mouthful of his beer and stood up also, leaving the bottle teetering on the edge of one of the sailing magazines.

Aware of the obvious dangers, Grace had to steel herself not to lean down and rescue it before it fell over and sprayed sticky liquid over the table and the rug below.

Instead, she moved towards the door, avoiding Connolly's narrow-eyed appraisal, desperate to get out of there before Sean could embarrass her again.

But unfortunately he wasn't quite finished.

Looking at Jack, he said, 'We're going to have a proper catch-up, old buddy.' He tried to catch Grace's arm, but she'd already moved out of his reach. 'How about next weekend?' he added. 'I've got to go back to London tomorrow, but I'll try to get up again on Friday evening. What do you say?'

'Well…'

Jack was non-committal. The last thing he wanted was another awkward interlude like this.

'I'd like to tell you my ideas about developing the website,' Sean continued. 'It might be something you'd be interested in. I'd be glad to give you all the details.'

Grace wanted to groan.

She'd been half afraid Sean had been about to bring that up earlier on. As soon as he'd heard that Jack was living in the village, Sean's intentions had been clear.

Jack straightened away from the bureau. He was watching them both through those narrowed eyes, his absurdly thick lashes veiling their expression.

She thought she could guess what he was thinking. He knew exactly what was going on here. She just hoped he didn't think she had any part in it.

'Yeah,' he said at last, without enthusiasm, and, in spite of being innocent of any wrongdoing, Grace could feel the colour pouring into her face. 'I'll think about it.'

Grace crossed the hall, wondering how she could have been foolish enough to believe Sean thought of anyone but himself. All she'd succeeded in doing was making herself look equally avaricious, to a man who probably regarded both of them with contempt.

Jack's eyes were drawn to the unconsciously sensuous sway of Grace's hips as she headed towards the exit. The low-rise waistband of her jeans exposed a tempting glimpse of very fair skin. And, although he couldn't be absolutely certain, he thought she had a small tattoo etched in the hollow of her spine.

She glanced back once and their eyes met, and Jack felt a momentary twinge of guilt. He had no right to be staring at the girl, no right to be thinking thoughts about her he'd believed he'd never have again.

But, no matter what restrictions he might put upon his conscience, he couldn't deny she was a very sexy lady…

Grace left the Bay Horse with a feeling of relief.

It was good to be home; good to be staying with her parents again. But it had been an extremely frustrating day.

In her room at the pub, the noise from the bar had been penetrating. She wasn't used to the social atmosphere of the Bay Horse these days. And even with the television playing, she could still hear the rumble of men's voices, the shouts of laughter, the sound of car doors slamming in the parking area outside.

And because of this, she intended to find herself other lodgings. Her parents would be disappointed, no doubt, but she was used to living on her own.

Besides, getting herself a small apartment would prove to her parents that she was serious about leaving London. It might also help to get Sean Nesbitt off her back.

It was a pleasant evening, and she'd decided to take a walk. Her mother was resting. Since her bout with breast cancer and the subsequent course of chemotherapy, Mrs Spencer was easily tired and rested often. Evidently the sounds of the pub didn't trouble her.

Grace chose to walk down to the harbour. She hadn't visited the quayside since her return and it used to be a favourite haunt of hers. She was hoping it might help to put the problems of the day into perspective.

She'd wasted the morning at an old vicarage not far from Rothburn, waiting for a client who hadn't shown.

Then, in the afternoon, she'd had to fend off the advances of a property developer.

William Grafton, who was in his late forties, had expressed an interest in some dilapidated cottages that were for sale on the coast. It was an isolated spot, but he'd said he thought they might be suitable for conversion to holiday lets. The area was a Mecca for birdwatchers and other naturalists, and accommodation was limited.

Now, however, Grace wondered if that had only been a ploy. He'd come into the agency to see her boss, but as soon as he'd recognised Grace he'd switched his attention to her.

She shook her head. Had he really thought she might be interested in him? A married man, moreover, who was old enough to be her father?

Grace had found herself wondering if she was cut out to be an estate agent, after all. Maybe she should try to find a job in a library or doing research. Something that tested her academic rather than her people skills.

Pulling the hairband out of her hair, she tipped back her head to allow the mass of red-gold curls to tumble about her shoulders.

Gosh, that felt good. Even the headache that had been probing at her temples for the past hour was eased by the removal of the confining band.

She hadn't realised it before, but she was still tense from having to deal with William Grafton. The man was a menace, she thought, irritably. Mr Hughes could speak to him next time he came into the agency.

The trouble was he was also a friend of her father's. And a patron of the Bay Horse. And as he was a client of the agency, she had to avoid offending him on three counts.

Leaving the forecourt of the pub, she started down the hill towards the seafront. Rothburn now had a thriving marina, catering to all kinds of leisure craft.

Was this where Jack Connolly kept his boat?

The thought came out of nowhere and she hurriedly flicked it away. She'd reached the quayside now, and she refused to let thoughts of Jack Connolly spoil the evening for her.

The area wasn't busy. The fishing quay was littered with lobster pots and wooden boxes, evidence of the sale that had been held there earlier in the day. But there were few people about.

The marina itself was separated from the working side of the operation by a stone pier. It ran out to a small lighthouse that marked the entrance to the harbour. Rows of slips provided mooring for a surprising number of vessels; small yachts and sailing dinghies rubbing shoulders with larger, ocean-going, craft.

Grace had always liked the idea of sailing. When she was younger, she used to tell her father she was going to be a fisherman herself when she grew up.

Until he'd taken her out on one of the small trawlers and the swell had made her sick.

She half smiled at the memory and exchanged a greeting with an old man sitting on one of the capstans, smoking his pipe. She'd known the man since she was a toddler, she realised. That was the thing about Rothburn: everybody knew who you were.

Resting her arms on the railings that ran along one side of the pier, she scanned the boats moored in the slips with more than a casual eye.

She refused to acknowledge she was curious about the kind of boat a man like Jack Connolly might own. Probably the most expensive, she thought ruefully. Like that gleaming cruiser, with at least three decks.

'Looking for something?'

CHAPTER THREE

GRACE STARTED ALMOST GUILTILY.

Despite the quietness of her surroundings, she hadn't heard anyone's approach and, glancing down, she could see why. He was wearing canvas boots, their rubber soles almost silent on the stone jetty.

Taking a deep breath, she turned.

'Mr Connolly,' she said politely. 'How nice to see you again.'

'Is it?'

Jack regarded her from between narrowed lids, wondering why he'd chosen to speak to her at all. Not ten days ago, he'd been hoping he'd never have to see her or her boyfriend again.

Grace lifted slim shoulders. She was still wearing the cream shell and navy suit she'd worn for work and, compared to his short-sleeved tee and black jeans, she felt ridiculously overdressed.

'I...was just on my way home,' she lied and saw the way his mobile mouth turned down.

Clearly, he didn't believe her, but she couldn't help that. She had no reason to care what he thought of her. But she couldn't deny that she was powerfully aware of him as a man.

Still, for the present, she had to pretend that she

and Sean were still together. She'd been in danger of denying that fact when she was at Jack's house.

'A pity,' he remarked now, taking up a position similar to the one she had adopted. Lean muscled arms rested on the rail only inches from the hand she'd been using to support herself. 'I thought maybe you were looking for the *Osprey*.'

'The *Osprey*?'

Trying to ignore the fact that his soft Irish accent stroked like velvet over her skin, Grace managed to sound amazingly bewildered. So much so that Jack turned his head sideways to look at her.

'Yeah, the *Osprey*,' he said. 'My boat.'

'Oh—' Grace moistened her lips. For some reason she was feeling a little breathless and tried to hide it. 'Of—of course.' Did she sound convincing? 'I'd forgotten you had a boat.'

Jack made a sound that was half groan, half laugh. 'Yeah, right,' he said, and suddenly she resented his mockery.

'Yes,' she declared tightly. 'Or do you imagine I came here looking for your boat? Perhaps you even think I was hoping to see you.'

'Hey…' He sounded almost amused now. 'What did I say? I just thought—'

'Yes, I know what you thought, Mr Connolly,' retorted Grace hotly. 'I've met men like you before.'

'I'll bet.' Jack straightened, his own expression sobering. 'I was being polite, that's all. Forget it.' He straightened. 'See you around.'

He turned to stride away along the pier and instantly Grace felt ashamed.

It was evidently her day for annoying people, she thought resignedly, and Jack had every right to be annoyed with her.

For heaven's sake, what had he said? It wasn't his fault that the man had a talent for getting under her skin.

'Mr Conn—I mean, Jack!'

Cursing her high-heeled pumps, Grace hurried after him. The stonework was uneven in places and she'd ricked her ankle at least twice before he stopped and looked back.

Immediately, Grace slowed to a walk, supremely self-conscious as she approached him. He didn't say anything. His lean dark face was closed; enigmatic. And so incredibly sensual, she half regretted giving him a second chance.

'Um—I just wanted to say I'm sorry,' she said, trying to sound cool and confident. 'It's been a long day. I'm afraid you took the brunt.'

Jack surveyed her silently. Like her, he was conscious of the fact that there was more going on here than a simple apology. He guessed she felt obliged to be civil to him because of Sean Nesbitt. If only she knew.

For his part, he was far too aware of the full breasts rising and falling rapidly beneath her silk top. The top was less revealing than the tee shirt had been, but no less sexy.

She was wearing a short-skirted suit, too, that exposed more of those long, spectacular legs. Were her legs bare? He thought so. And the notion of running his hands up them and under her skirt was as unwelcome as his reaction.

As she drew nearer the fragrance of her perfume drifted to him. It was light, flowery, with just an underlying trace of musk. No doubt her sudden exertion was responsible for the wave of heat that was rising up her throat and into her cheeks.

'It's okay,' he said, when she stopped beside him, managing to sound relaxed even though he was far from it. 'I've had days like that.' He paused, and then, because something more was required, 'How's the job?'

'All right.' Grace shrugged. 'I guess.'

The pause was significant.

'You only guess?'

His dark brows ascended and Grace pulled a wry face. 'Working in Alnwick is great, but I'm not sure if I'm cut out to be an estate agent,' she admitted. 'I'm not a saleswoman.'

Jack pushed his thumbs into the back waistband of his jeans and regarded her sympathetically. 'You haven't been doing it for very long,' he said. 'How do you know?'

Grace sighed. 'This is my second week.'

'So give it more time.'

'I suppose I'll have to.'

Jack thought he sounded amazingly reasonable

in the circumstances. But, since Lisa had died, he'd considered himself immune from the opposite sex. And he had been until this girl came into his orbit. He didn't like feeling unsure of himself, but he was.

The urge to tuck a strand of silky red-gold hair behind her ear was almost irresistible. He wanted to touch her, to feel the satin-smooth skin beneath his fingers.

His muscles tightened automatically in anticipation, but somehow he reined his feelings in.

She was waiting for him to go on, so he said deliberately, 'What does Sean think?'

'Oh, Sean…'

If Jack hadn't been so sure he was attributing her with feelings she didn't have, he'd have said she sounded fed up.

'Sean doesn't know,' she said at last. 'I haven't discussed it with him.' And nor would she. She took a breath. 'Yet.'

Jack nodded, and she wondered what he was thinking. Despite this conversation, she didn't think he had a lot of respect for her or for Sean.

Well, that was okay, she decided. She'd had it with attractive Irishmen. With any man, for that matter. And just because Connolly was being sympathetic didn't mean she should trust him, either.

'So what do you plan to do?' he asked now, rocking back on his heels. 'If you left the estate agency, what sort of job would you like?'

'I haven't thought about it.' Which was true. And

despite her determination not to get involved with this man, it would be so easy to confide in him.

Her shoulders stiffening, she continued, 'I suppose I'll think about it.' She paused. 'I intend to stay in Rothburn. My mother likes me being nearer at hand. We've always been a close family.'

'You have brothers and sisters?'

'No. I'm an only child.'

'And that's the real reason you want to stay? Because of your mother?'

'What is this? An interrogation?' She moved towards the railings, her fingers curling over the cold metal. Then she sighed. 'I suppose I want to stay here, too.'

O—kay.

Jack gave in to the impulse to go and join her. Where was the harm? he thought, leaning on the rail beside her. The fact that Grace was evidently conscious of his bare arm only inches from her sleeve was a bonus.

Dear God, he was in lust, and that was so not good.

'How is your mother, anyway?'

Jack's voice was a little strained, but he couldn't help it. He'd chosen the words purposely to get his mind off the delights of the slender body almost brushing his sleeve.

It wasn't working, so he added tersely, 'I'm sorry. I should have asked you before.'

'Why?' Wide green eyes turned to look at him.

'You don't know my mother, do you? I asked Dad, and he said that as far as he knew——'

Her voice trailed off in confusion. Oh, God, why had she admitted she'd been asking her father about him? But she had to finish her sentence. 'He——um—— he said you'd never been into the pub.'

'I haven't.'

Jack didn't sound perturbed, but Grace was mortified.

'I suppose my enquiry stems from the fact that she's your mother,' he went on reasonably. 'I hope you didn't think I was prying.'

Prying?

Grace swallowed a little convulsively. 'She's—— she's much better,' she said. 'Cancer takes some getting over. But thank you for asking.'

Jack shrugged, turning his gaze towards the marina. But he could still see her eyes, open and candid, those words like a mirror to her soul.

Sean was so lucky, he thought, whereas he was being less than honest with her. And he had no right to be provocative. It couldn't be easy for her and Sean to spend so much time apart.

All the same, he couldn't deny that Grace's mouth was so soft, so generous. A mouth he would very much like to taste...

Not that he ever would, he assured himself grimly. He was celibate, he reminded himself. And he intended to stay that way.

But there was nothing wrong with a little abstract speculation, was there?

Abstract?

Dragging his mind out of the gutter, he forced a polite smile. 'So do you think Sean will like living in Rothburn?' he asked, even though the idea of them setting up home somewhere in the vicinity filled him with dismay.

'Oh...' Grace was grateful to be distracted from her own thoughts. 'Sean likes living in London.' And that was true. She pushed herself away from the rail. 'We'll see.'

Jack turned his back to the barrier, arms spread along the rail where she'd been leaning, hooking one foot onto a lower rung.

He'd been on the verge of saying, *Let me know what he decides,* but it was really nothing to do with him. Besides, hadn't he wanted to avoid Sean in the future? It would be a hell of a lot safer if they both moved away.

'I'd better go.'

Grace was uneasily aware of how disturbing Jack looked lounging against the rail. He was much broader than Sean and, with his arms spread wide, his chest looked strong and muscular.

His stomach was flat, powerful thighs taut against the fabric of his jeans. Jeans that were worn to a much lighter shade in places, places where Grace determined not to look.

Although she did.

She couldn't stop herself. The impressive bulge between his legs couldn't help but draw her gaze. She felt an unfamiliar shivery sensation in the pit of her stomach.

Which troubled her a lot.

She blew out a breath.

'Goodbye.'

With a nervous lift of her hand, she started back along the pier towards the quayside. But she was intensely conscious of Jack's eyes watching her, of how much less constrained she'd have felt if she hadn't been wearing a skirt.

'Goodbye, Grace.'

The careless farewell drifted after her and she had to steel herself not to turn around and look back.

Jack spent the following weekend half anticipating that Sean would find an excuse to come and visit him again. But, despite his fears, Saturday and Sunday passed without incident.

And he didn't know whether to be glad or sorry.

He knew he wouldn't have objected to seeing Grace again, but it was probably just as well to cool that thought. In any case, he'd spent a goodly portion of both days on his boat, so it was possible he'd missed any visitors. Although knowing Sean, he doubted his temporary absence would have deterred him.

It poured with rain Monday and Tuesday and even Wednesday morning was overcast.

His housekeeper had phoned to say she wouldn't be in that morning. And, unusually, Jack was feeling housebound. With the redecoration complete, and no other restoration project in prospect, he was restless.

Emptying the remains of his coffee into the sink, he left the kitchen and headed upstairs to his bedroom. He'd take the car for a drive, he decided firmly. He felt like driving and there was nothing to keep him here.

'Are you going out?'

Jack was zipping up a pair of khaki pants when Lisa's voice interrupted his thoughts.

He turned to find her slim form balanced on the edge of the windowsill. And he thought how typical it was that she hadn't appeared for over a week, but now that he was planning on going out, she had to interfere.

'Yeah, why not?' He turned to pick up his leather jacket off the bed. 'I've got nothing better to do.'

Lisa sniffed. 'You could get a job.' She paused, pressing a scarlet-tipped nail to her lips. 'You have too much spare time on your hands.'

'And that's my fault, is it?'

Lisa's lips pursed thoughtfully. 'You're going to see that girl, aren't you?'

Jack's jaw dropped. 'I beg your pardon?'

'Don't pretend you don't know who I'm talking about.'

Lisa slipped down off the windowsill and limped

on her one high heel across the earth-toned carpet. 'Even so, I doubt if Father Michael would approve.'

Jack's lips twitched with humour now. Father Michael had been the priest who'd married them. He'd also officiated at Lisa's funeral, but he doubted she was referring to that.

'I think Father Michael gave up on me a good time ago,' he remarked at last. 'And I'm sure he'd be the first to suggest I should move on with my life.'

Lisa looked doubtful. 'She's very attractive, I suppose.'

Jack shook his head. 'Do I have to remind you she already has a boyfriend?'

'You mean Sean Nesbitt?'

'That's right. Sean Nesbitt. He's a mate. I'm not about to forget that, am I?'

Lisa pulled a face. 'Really?'

'Hey, I don't tell lies,' retorted Jack, slotting his wallet and his mobile phone into his jacket pockets. 'Which reminds me, you never did tell me where you were going the night you had the accident.'

He didn't get an answer and he didn't really expect one. It was a question he'd asked many times before. He knew, without even looking again, that Lisa was gone.

The Lexus was still standing on the drive and, dodging the rain, Jack got behind the wheel and started the powerful engine. Then, shoving a CD into the player, he backed the vehicle out onto the road.

So far he'd only seen a small part of the area. Cumbria and the Lake District were only a couple of hours' drive west but, without much hesitation, Jack headed for the A1.

As he drove Jack wondered if he'd intended to visit Alnwick all along or whether Lisa's taunts had piqued his interest. Either way, he refused to concede that he had any anticipation of seeing Grace again.

He was lucky enough to get parked in the town centre.

Despite the lowering clouds, there were plenty of people about, and Jack bought a map of the area before retiring to the nearest coffee shop to study it.

'Looking for somewhere in particular?'

The pretty waitress who'd served him his coffee was standing at his shoulder and Jack looked up at her ruefully, wishing he had an answer for that.

'Not specially,' he replied non-committally. 'I've never been to Alnwick before.'

'Oh, you're a tourist!' The girl evidently thought she had him taped. 'You're from Ireland, aren't you?' She smiled flirtatiously. 'I love your accent.'

'Thanks.' Jack grinned, amused in spite of himself. 'Do you live in Alnwick?'

'Just outside.' She pulled a face. 'It's too expensive to live in town.'

'It is?'

'Oh, God, yes.' She glanced over her shoulder to make sure the proprietor of the café hadn't noticed she was wasting time. 'It's just as well you're not looking for a house.' She dimpled. 'Unless you're a secret millionaire, of course.'

Jack looked down at the map again, not wanting to give her any ideas. Besides, he reminded himself, he hadn't come here looking for property.

Or estate agents, if it came to that.

'Are you staying in town?'

The girl was persistent and Jack decided he had to nip this in the bud.

'No,' he said neutrally, swallowing the last of his coffee and pulling out his wallet. 'I'm heading north to—' He cast a quick glance at the map. 'To Bamburgh.' He got to his feet. 'I believe there's a castle there, too.'

'Are you interested in castles?'

When Jack started for the counter to pay his bill, she accompanied him, apparently indifferent to the customers still waiting to be served.

Avoiding a direct answer, he said, 'Thanks for your advice.' He accepted his change with an apologetic smile for the cashier, hoping he could get out of the café without offending the waitress hovering behind him.

But to his dismay, she followed him to the door.

'If you need someone to show you around, I'll be finished in an hour,' she offered eagerly. And Jack was just about to break his own rules and blow her off when the door opened and another young woman came in.

'Jack!'

'Grace.'

Jack managed to keep his reaction under control. But he was fairly sure that Grace had immediately regretted the way his name had sprung so effortlessly to her lips.

However, it was the young waitress who looked the most put out.

'Hi, Grace,' she said grudgingly. Then, glancing at Jack, 'Do you two know one another?'

'Um—a little.'

Grace was offhand, and before Jack could say anything in his own defence the waitress spoke again.

'Hey,' she exclaimed disbelievingly. 'Don't tell me this is your boyfriend. I thought his name was Sean.'

In the circumstances, Grace was loath to say anything. She felt hot colour rising up into her face. Of all people to run into—again—it had to be Jack Connolly. And, judging from the other girl's attitude, she wouldn't be averse to him taking an interest in her.

And why should it bother her? thought Grace crossly.

Meanwhile, Jack was feeling significantly peeved. He was all too aware of how the situation must look to Grace and he didn't like it.

'Look, I'm leaving,' he said, uncaring at that moment what either of them thought of him. He nodded to Grace. 'See you around.'

CHAPTER FOUR

GRACE CAME OUT of the café a few minutes later carrying three cups of cappuccino in a paper sack and a bag containing the sugary pastries Mr Hughes was partial to.

She didn't enjoy this part of her job. But being the youngest in the agency, she was expected to do the coffee run. She supposed it was better than having to make it herself, but there were days, like today, when she had other things to think about.

Like explaining to William Grafton why his offer for the cottages at Culworth had been rejected.

She wasn't looking forward to that, either, but Mr Hughes had been adamant that it was her responsibility.

'You have to learn to handle awkward clients, Grace,' he'd told her firmly. 'In an agency like ours, we can't just pick and choose.'

She could have said that handling awkward clients was the least of it. Handling a man who could lose her her job—however undesirable that job might be—was something else.

She glanced about her a little apprehensively as she crossed the street to the agency. But to her relief there was no sign of Jack Connolly waiting outside.

There was a big Lexus parked across the square

that she thought might belong to him. But the vehicle was empty. Which was probably just as well.

Probably?

Impatient with herself for even doubting that scenario, she pushed open the door of the agency and stepped inside.

Only to find Jack Connolly standing in the reception area, showing every appearance of being interested in the properties displayed on the walls.

Not that she'd be expected to deal with him, she saw, with mixed feelings. Standing just beyond Jack was William Grafton, his broad, smug features lighting up when he saw her.

'Grace,' he exclaimed, and Grace was aware that his use of her name had attracted Jack's attention. 'I've been waiting for you. Grant tells me you have some news for me.'

Grace took a deep breath. Then, setting Elizabeth Fleming's coffee on her desk, she did the same with her own before heading for the private office where Grant Hughes worked.

'I won't be a minute, Mr Grafton,' she said, wondering if her day could get any worse.

By the time she'd given Mr Hughes his coffee and doughnuts, Elizabeth Fleming, Mr Hughes's assistant, had left her desk to attend to Jack personally. The two of them were currently huddled cosily beside a free-standing display.

William Grafton, meanwhile, had seated himself in the clients' chair beside her desk.

'Well?' Grafton said as soon as she was seated, and Grace took the opportunity to take a sip of her coffee before getting down to business.

She needed the boost of caffeine, and if Grafton didn't like it, it was just too bad.

'Grant says you've heard from the vendor,' he prompted, when she didn't immediately answer him. 'I hope it's good news.'

Grace sighed. 'I'm afraid not, Mr Grafton. The offer you made has been rejected.' She paused, consulting the papers on her desk, as if she needed confirmation of what she already knew. 'Mrs Naughton wants considerably more than you offered for the properties.'

Grafton snorted, once again drawing Jack's attention.

Despite his apparent absorption in what Mrs Fleming was saying, he was evidently listening to their conversation, too.

'Those cottages are practically dropping to bits,' Grafton exclaimed, his blunt fist coming down hard on Grace's desk, dispelling any other thoughts. 'The old woman knows that. This is just a ploy to get me to offer more.'

He scowled across the desk. 'I want you to get in touch with her again and tell her it's not going to work. She's not dealing with some amateur, you know. When William Grafton wants something, he gets it. You tell her that.'

'Mr Grafton—'

'You heard what I said.'

Rudely, Grafton thrust back his chair, the legs scraping noisily over the wooden floor. Then, after adjusting the collar of his oilskin jacket, he leant forward again.

'You sort this out, Grace, there's a good girl. I'm relying on you.' He tapped his nose with his forefinger. 'No one ever said William Grafton wasn't a generous man. Know what I mean?' He started towards the door. 'Don't let me down.'

Grace could hardly contain her anger. The patronising man! How dared he call her 'a good girl'? And he actually expected her to be flattered because he was giving her his business.

She caught her breath and, as she did so, she was made aware that Jack Connolly must have heard what was said, as well. And how humiliating was that?

All the same, she had to wonder what he was doing here. She didn't believe in coincidence. He must have come here deliberately.

But why?

To see her?

The idea was provocative. And exciting.

But she couldn't let him see how she was feeling. He had a bad enough opinion of her as it was.

She took a generous gulp of her coffee and got to her feet just as Elizabeth Fleming approached her desk.

'Have you a minute, Grace?'

Grace blew out a breath. 'Um—yes. Sure.' She tamped down a feeling of apprehension. 'How can I help?'

Elizabeth gave her a rueful smile. A middle-aged woman, in her late fifties, she'd been kind to Grace, easing her introduction to the agency and generally being on hand if she was needed.

'Those cottages,' she said in a low voice. 'The ones at Culworth. Are they still for sale?'

Grace blinked. 'You mean the cottages Mr Grafton offered for?'

'I'm afraid so.' Elizabeth pulled a wry face. 'I assume you've told Mr Grafton his offer was declined.'

'Well, yes.' Grace's brows drew together. 'He wants me to speak to Mrs Naughton again.'

'Has he increased his offer?'

'No.'

'I see.' Elizabeth pulled her lower lip between her teeth. 'Well, I'm pretty sure if that's the case Mrs Naughton won't be interested.'

Grace sighed. 'I did try to tell him that.'

'I'm sure you did.' Elizabeth frowned. 'The thing is I've got another client who'd like to view them.'

'To view the cottages?'

Grace's eyes went automatically to Jack, but his face was expressionless.

Not that she was deceived. He had obviously heard what she and Grafton had been talking about. Heavens, she *knew* he had. What on earth was he playing at?

'Yes.' Elizabeth was going on, completely unaware of Grace's agitation. 'But unfortunately I've got the Lawsons coming at twelve o'clock. I don't have time to go out to Culworth this morning, and Mr Connolly wants to see the cottages today.'

Does he?

Grace bit her lip, trying not to let Elizabeth see how uneasy she was.

'So—what?' she asked tightly. 'Do you want me to go?'

'Would you?' Elizabeth looked relieved. 'I'd be really grateful.' She paused. 'I mean, it may come to nothing, but apparently Mr Connolly's an architect and he's looking for development property in the area.' She grimaced. 'I'd love it if you could tell William Grafton that Mrs Naughton has had another offer.'

Grace would love that, too, she admitted wryly. She had few illusions that Jack was serious, but she couldn't let Elizabeth down, so, with a rueful smile, she said, 'Okay. I'll do it.' She turned to pick up her coffee. 'I hope… Mr Connolly…has his own transport.'

As if she didn't know that Jack's Lexus was parked on the square outside.

'Oh, I'm sure he has.'

Elizabeth turned back to speak to her client, and Grace swallowed the remains of her coffee.

Okay, she thought, he wouldn't be the first client

she'd had whose intentions might be less than honourable, but she assured herself she could handle it.

And she was probably wrong, anyway.

Feeling eyes upon her, she looked up to find Jack watching her. And chided herself for the sudden frisson of excitement that zinged along her nerves at his cool-eyed stare.

She turned away, but the image of his dark, good-looking face and lean muscled frame stayed with her as she gathered her handbag from the drawer and slipped on her olive-green jacket.

'Mr Connolly has his own car.'

Elizabeth was back at her side, her anxious expression an indication that she wasn't totally unaware of Grace's reluctance to deal with this client.

She moistened her lips. 'Are you all right, Grace?'

'Good. I'm good.' Grace forced a smile. 'Does— does Mr Connolly know the way to Culworth?'

'He says he'll follow you,' said Elizabeth at once. She sighed. 'You know, I would take him myself if it weren't for the Lawsons—'

'I know.' Grace managed to infuse a little more enthusiasm into her voice. 'I'm grateful for your confidence in me. Is Mr Connolly ready to go now?'

'I'm ready.'

Grace had been unaware of Jack's approach, and his low attractive voice caused another shiver to feather her spine.

Elizabeth turned to him with obvious pleasure. 'Miss Spencer will take care of you,' she said, patting Grace's arm encouragingly. 'I'll see you later, right?'

'Right.'

Jack nodded, and Grace was obliged to pick up her handbag and precede him across the room and out of the door.

She waited until they were out of hearing distance and then turned impatiently towards him.

'Just what do you think you're doing?'

Jack's dark brows rose at the obvious accusation in her voice.

'I understood we were going to view a row of run-down cottages at some place called Culworth. Isn't that right?'

Grace sighed. 'Like you're interested in seeing a row of derelict cottages.'

Jack pushed his thumbs into the front pockets of his khakis. 'I am.'

Grace stared at him frustratedly, wishing she didn't have this almost visceral awareness of his masculinity. She struggled to suppress those totally unwelcome feelings and said, 'Why would you be interested in the Culworth cottages? You're not a property developer. It's kind of you to try to help me deal with Mr Grafton, but he's not likely to go away just because someone else has shown an interest.'

'I know that.'

Jack conceded the point, not altogether comfortable with his reasons for getting involved. But when he'd heard Grafton, mouthing off about what he wanted Grace to do, he'd known an immediate urge to thwart the man, any way he could.

'But I am an architect,' he went on mildly. 'With time on my hands.' He paused. 'It occurred to me that buying another property and developing it—'

'There are *six* cottages,' broke in Grace helplessly, but Jack only lifted his shoulders in a dismissive gesture.

'So? It will be a challenge.'

Grace shook her head. 'You don't mean that.'

'Don't I?' Jack shrugged. 'Forgive me if I think I know my own mind better than you do.'

His words were cooler now, reminding her that she was still an employee of the agency. Whatever her personal feelings might be, Mr Hughes wouldn't be pleased if she inadvertently offended another possible valuable client.

'All right.' Grace pursed her lips. 'I'll get my car.'

Jack's dark eyes assessed her. 'Or we could both go in mine,' he offered evenly, but she just gave him a speaking look.

'I don't think, so,' she said stiffly, looping the strap of her bag over her shoulder. 'I'm parked at the back of the agency. Just give me a couple of minutes to bring my car round.'

Jack made a gesture of assent, wondering seriously why he was doing this. And she was right. This wasn't why he'd come to Alnwick.

Pushing his hands into his jacket pockets, he watched her walk away with a feeling of irritation.

He even played with the idea of just getting into his car and driving away, but he knew he wouldn't do that.

For some reason, the rigid cut of her spine and the provocative sway of her hips assaulted his senses. It was crazy, because she was so obviously not interested in him, either as a client, or a friend. And anything else...

But he arrested his thoughts there before they took him places he really didn't want to go. Well, not in the middle of Alnwick High Street, he mused drily as a small red Civic turned the corner at the end of the block and drove towards him.

It was Grace, and, grateful for the distraction, Jack strode across the square and climbed behind the wheel of the Lexus. His eyes met Grace's briefly, and then, with a courteous wave of his hand, he allowed her to lead the way.

They drove north for a couple of miles before turning towards the sea. It appeared at fleeting intervals as the road wound through a series of hidden bends and blind summits to a small hamlet perched on cliffs above a rocky cove.

Culworth.

Jack read the sign without surprise, following the little Civic past a ruined church to where a gravelled area provided a place to park.

Grace pulled in ahead of him and Jack edged the Lexus in behind. Then, switching off the engine, he glanced around.

Their arrival had caused a flurry of black birds to rise out of the crumbling walls of the church and circle excitedly above them.

'Crows!' said Grace, thrusting open her door and getting out just as Jack did the same.

Long legs, corded with muscle, attracted her unwilling eyes. And, as he came towards her, she was uneasily aware of how big he was compared to Sean. Of the casual way he pushed back his hair, of the faint humour tugging at his mouth.

Jack glanced up at the birds. 'Talk about omens,' he said drily. 'Almost scared the hell out of me.'

Grace thought it would take something a lot more frightening than a few birds to scare Jack Connolly, but she let it go.

Instead, adopting her most businesslike tone, she said, 'If you'll follow me, I'll show you where the cottages are situated.'

'Right.'

Jack fell in beside her as she started along a narrow lane that ran beside the church wall. The wind off the sea was funnelled by the wall and the trees facing it.

Meanwhile, for Grace, having Jack Connolly walking beside her was causing a definite rise in her temperature.

Impatient with herself, Grace walked faster than her heels allowed, and almost ricked her ankle in the process.

'You okay?'

Jack had noticed, and Grace sighed.

'Fine,' she said shortly. And then, because she hadn't spoken since they left the cars, 'It's not much further.'

They passed one or two free-standing cottages that obviously still had tenants, and a boarded-up schoolhouse that just as obviously didn't.

The road forked and Grace turned onto the lane that cut across the cliff. Ahead of them, Jack could see what he assumed were the cottages in question. A row of narrow buildings with peeling paintwork and broken windows forming an uneven terrace.

He guessed that the position of the cottages was their main advantage. They had an uninterrupted view of the coastline and the wild and beautiful sea beyond.

Grace glanced up at him as they reached the first of the cottages and said drily, 'Not what you imagined, I expect.'

Jack pulled his hands out of his pockets and pushed back his tousled hair. 'Can we go inside?' he asked, without answering her, and Grace shrugged.

'It will be very dirty,' she said, fumbling in her bag for the set of keys. 'The roofs leak and the rain drives through the broken windows.'

'Yeah, I had guessed that.' Jack regarded her with raised brows. 'Is this your usual way of encouraging a sale?'

Grace had to smile. 'Not usually,' she admitted, brushing past him to open the first gate. It stuck—

of course!—but by leaning her weight against it, she managed to get it open. Then she walked swiftly up the path to the front door.

She found the key she wanted without difficulty, but as she opened the door she noticed the damp dirty stain on the jacket of her olive-green suit.

It must have happened when she leant on the gate. She pressed her lips together as she pushed open the door. She should have asked Jack to open the gate. It served her right for behaving like a shrew.

Holding her bag in such a way that it hid the stain, she stepped inside. Straight into a pool of icy water.

And she'd thought the day couldn't get any worse.

Her involuntary shriek of alarm caused Jack to abandon his surveillance of the outside of the cottages. Striding up the path, he stepped into the cottage after her, narrowly avoiding the broken floorboard where the rainwater had gathered.

Of course!

'It's okay.' Grace was already regretting her instinctive outburst. She moved away from the entrance, aware that her black suede pumps were probably ruined. 'I just got a bit of a shock, that's all.'

'What happened?'

Jack was regarding her intently, the concern in his dark eyes clearly visible in the light from the open doorway.

Grace quivered, sure that his sympathy wasn't genuine. And wished she weren't wondering how she would feel if it were.

'Oh—I just stepped in a puddle, that's all,' she said, turning to survey the inside of the cottage.

More peeling paint, wallpaper torn and stained with dampness, a staircase that looked as if it wouldn't take their weight if they tried to use it.

'Are you sure you're all right?'

When she glanced round, Jack was still regarding her with doubtful eyes. And, dear Lord, she felt as if she were drowning in those deep and shadowy depths.

'I—I'm fine,' she assured him quickly, forcing herself to concentrate on the job in hand. 'Um—as you can see, the cottages need a complete renovation.' She managed a tight smile. 'It might be easier to knock them down and start over.'

'Oh, I wouldn't say that.'

Taking his cue from her, Jack made a preliminary examination of the entrance. The walls seemed sound enough, built years ago when breeze blocks weren't in common use. They needed pointing, of course, but if the foundations were solid, that wouldn't be a problem.

'But you have to admit, it's a lot of work,' said Grace, doubtfully. 'Mr Grafton seemed to think there might be rising damp.'

'And he would know,' said Jack wryly, his humour causing Grace to smile again in spite of herself.

'Well, at least he's a proper builder,' she retorted staunchly. 'Not someone only pretending to be interested for reasons of his own.'

'Is that what you think I'm doing?' Jack sucked in a breath. 'Do you think I'm wasting your time?'

'Well, aren't you?'

Grace didn't back down, even though she wanted to.

In an unexpected move, Jack backed up and closed the door, cutting off the chilling breeze off the sea.

Immediately, the light in the hall was narrowed to the broken fanlight above his head. It made the hall seem dark and claustrophobic, and Grace swallowed apprehensively.

'Do you imagine I'm only doing this because of some personal interest I have in you, Grace?'

CHAPTER FIVE

'I— No!'

Grace realised she was in a corner, both meta-phorically and physically, and she searched wildly for something to say.

'Um—Mr Grafton has already made an offer for the cottages,' she said valiantly. 'I'm supposed to be contacting the vendor at this moment to try to ne-gotiate a sale.'

'Yeah, I heard.'

Jack moved away from the door and, turning, Grace fairly bolted for the kitchen at the end of the hall.

The cottages were simple affairs, with only a front room and kitchen downstairs, and two bedrooms upstairs. But there was another door opening from the kitchen into a backyard, which offered an escape route should she feel she needed one.

'And do you think Mrs—North, was it?—will eventually accept Mr Grafton's offer?' asked Jack, pausing in the doorway from the hall.

His shoulder was propped against the splintered frame and, despite his dingy surroundings, he man-aged to look both darkly attractive and dangerous.

And in control.

But she wasn't. And her voice was shriller than it

should have been when she said, 'It's Mrs Naughton. And I think the rest is privileged information.'

Jack shrugged, remembering what he'd heard in the agency. Hardly privileged.

'Okay.' He chose not to argue. 'I can live with that. Do you mind if I take a look around?'

He straightened and was instantly aware of her stiffening. She was so tense; so uptight, dammit. What did she expect him to do to her?

He knew what he wanted to do, of course, but that was more privileged information. Nevertheless, he refused to back down at the first obstacle.

'Well, this is the downstairs area?'

It took a minute, but Jack belatedly remembered what he'd asked before his libido took over.

'Downstairs, upstairs, I'd like to see it all,' he said, aware of his own frustration. He regarded her with grudging eyes. 'You do want to sell these properties, don't you?'

Grace straightened her spine. 'Of course I do.'

'You could have fooled me!'

Jack's accent was suddenly disturbingly acute, but Grace couldn't allow herself to be persuaded by its unconscious charm. Starting reluctantly towards him, she said, 'If you'll let me pass, I'll lead the way.'

Grace had never been upstairs before.

William Grafton had taken one look around and decided the insides of the cottages would have to be gutted. It was one of his reasons for reducing his offer; the fact that, according to him, all the inner walls were rotten with damp.

However, despite her reservations, Grace was obliged to behave as if the stairs were sound. If the steps were rickety, and they certainly seemed that way, she had to be the one to find out. Mr Hughes would definitely have something to say if she returned with the news that their newest client had broken his leg.

There'd been a smell of mould downstairs, but it was much worse upstairs. Grace was glad to concentrate on that rather than on the possible thoughts of the man following her.

What was he thinking? she wondered, intensely conscious of the shortness of her skirt. And of the heat that emanated from him, enveloping her in an uneasy combination of shaving lotion and man.

In the first bedroom she discovered why the air upstairs was so much more oppressive. Although the windows had been broken here, too, someone had stuffed a sheet of cardboard into the gap. And there were signs of unauthorised occupation in the empty fast-food cartons and chocolate wrappers strewn across the floor.

'Kids,' said Jack dismissively, when Grace gave an exclamation of surprise. 'I doubt it's squatters. I think they'd choose something a little more salubrious.'

'You think?' Grace was doubtful. 'I didn't come

upstairs with Mr Grafton, so I didn't know about this until now.'

Jack pulled a wry face. 'Hey, I believe you,' he said humorously, moving over to the window. He had to step over an old duvet someone had left on the floor to do so. 'I wouldn't want to go upstairs with him myself.'

Grace's lips compressed. 'You think you're so amusing, don't you, Mr Connolly?'

Jack sighed. 'It's not usually such an effort,' he retorted drily. 'Can we make some progress here?'

Grace's expression didn't change. 'Progress towards what exactly?'

'Well, you're not making friends and influencing people,' remarked Jack, as a piece of the windowsill crumbled in his hand. 'For pity's sake, Grace, what have I done to make you treat me like a leper?'

'I'm not treating you like a leper.' Grace was defensive. 'I'm merely trying to do my job.'

'Yeah, right.' Patently he didn't believe her. 'Well, come here and see how dangerous this is. What's left of this window is in danger of falling on someone's head.'

Grace hesitated. 'No one ever comes here.'

'Well, someone does.' Jack indicated the debris on the floor. 'Perhaps you ought to inform your— what was it you called her?—your vendor? I dare say she'd be held responsible if somebody sustained a nasty cut or something worse.'

Grace caught her lower lip between her teeth.

Then, because it was her job after all, she made her way across the uneven floorboards to where Jack was waiting.

Jack showed her where the frame was crumbling. 'These kids—if it is kids—may be trespassing, but their parents would soon kick up a stink if one of them was badly injured.'

'Yes, that's true.'

Grace believed him. As someone with a law degree, she knew that where children were concerned judges tended to look elsewhere for someone to blame.

Like negligent owners, for example, with no warning signs or danger notices on display.

'I'll tell Mrs Naughton,' she said. 'It's really her responsibility.'

Jack turned to face her and she was immediately aware of how close he was. The heat emanating from his body enveloped her. She couldn't help but be sensitive to his maleness, to the raw sensual magnetism of the man.

Dear God!

She stepped back without thinking, her heel catching in the folds of the duvet lying on the floor behind her. She stumbled and would have fallen on her bottom if Jack hadn't quickly grabbed her flailing arms.

His hands were hard around her narrow biceps, strong hands that caught her and held her without obvious effort on his part.

His swift reaction brought her unceremoniously

against him. With her breasts crushed against his chest, she was sure he must be able to feel the pounding of her heart.

It was so unexpected. The whole incident left her breathless. Her hands were trapped between them, one thigh wedged intimately in the junction of his parted legs.

Jack expelled a sharp breath.

Dammit, this was so not meant to happen. Okay, he couldn't have let her fall on her butt. But he'd never intended her to fall into his arms. Or that he wouldn't want to let her go.

Pressed against him as she was, she seemed endearingly vulnerable. But that was crazy. It was only the shock she'd had that was stopping her from dragging herself away.

Nevertheless, with her curly hair brushing his chin and the faint flowery fragrance of her perfume assaulting his senses, she was utterly feminine. And he suspected the heated scent he could smell was the sudden warmth that skimmed her skin.

His mouth dried as he acknowledged that his racing pulse wasn't just the result of his exertion.

Grace tried to gather her scattered thoughts. Jack's breath was warm as it fanned her cheek and smelled not unpleasantly of coffee.

His body—now why was she thinking about his body?—felt lean and hard and disturbingly hot. When her hands fanned against his midriff, she could feel the heat of his skin through the fabric of his shirt.

And knew she should put some space between them.

She tilted her head and looked up into his dark compelling face and their eyes met.

And clung.

Jack's exclamation was harsh, but unmistakeably passionate. And when his hands tightened on her arms, she felt all the bones in her legs turn to water.

'We—we have to go,' she said, but her voice was thready and barely audible.

Jack nodded. 'Yeah,' he said hoarsely, but then he bent his head and covered her lips with his and she fairly melted against him.

Which was so wrong. But just at that moment it felt so incredibly right.

Jack thought his body might go up in flames. The yielding softness of her mouth beneath his was that devastating.

Her lips were moist, sensuous; igniting a flame inside him that was damn near irresistible. His hands slid down her arms and linked with hers. And it was the most natural thing in the world to wind her hands behind her back and urge her even closer against him.

Grace, meanwhile, could feel her senses slipping. What little resistance she had left was drifting away. And when Jack's tongue parted her lips and thrust hungrily into her mouth, she couldn't prevent her nails from digging urgently into his palms.

She was wearing a lemon silk shell beneath the jacket of her suit, a low-necked item that was so thin Jack could see the lacy curve of her demi-bra through it. He could also see the rounded swells of her breasts rising above it, the swollen nipples pressing against the lace.

Dammit, he wanted to touch her; to touch *them*. To slip his hand up under her top and caress skin that he guessed would be as dewy soft as her mouth.

But that was only part of it, he acknowledged grimly. What he really wanted to do was shove her up against the peeling plaster of this ugly room. To slide that sexy little skirt up her hips and bury the hard-on her hot little body had incited in that wet haven he knew he'd find between her legs.

He blew out a breath.

That wasn't going to happen.

Not in this lifetime; no way.

And the sooner he put a stop to this, the sooner he'd remember who he was; who *she* was.

Sean's girlfriend!

He had to kill these feelings that were so—unwanted?

Right.

With a determination that was enforced by the belief that Grace would blame him for this, Jack reluctantly released her hands and stepped away from her.

Not far, because the window was at his back. But far enough for her to realise what he was doing.

'Like you said,' he declared, his voice a little rough. He cleared his throat before continuing, 'We should go.'

It took a few moments for Grace to get her head round what was happening. She still felt dazed; disorientated. Half convinced she'd imagined the whole thing.

But as she looked about her she knew it was no illusion. It was real. Jack was real. And the tingling in her lips and—uncomfortably—between her legs brought the whole disturbing scene into sharp focus.

'I— Yes,' she said, her hand going automatically to her hair.

She could feel the knot she'd made that morning had come loose and fiery strands were tumbling about her shoulders.

She probably looked as loose as she felt, she thought painfully, struggling to restore her hair to some semblance of order. But her hands weren't quite steady and the pins refused to stay in place.

'Yes,' she said again, abandoning her efforts in favour of bending to pick up her handbag from the floor. She didn't know exactly when she'd dropped it, but she obviously had, and she imagined it was probably as worse for wear as she was.

She licked her lips, unconsciously provocative in spite of herself. 'I expect you've seen enough.'

Jack wondered if that was a serious comment.

'I think so,' he replied civilly, glad to feel his erection subsiding. Even as his own personal demon reminded him, rather mockingly, that there was a hell of a lot more he'd wanted to see.

They went down the stairs, Jack leading the way this time.

If it was a belated attempt to salvage his self-respect, he had few doubts that it was appreciated. And as soon as Grace had had the time to reconsider the events of the past half hour, he wouldn't get off so lightly.

Perhaps she'd even come to the conclusion that Mr Grafton wasn't so bad, after all.

'Was he interested?'

Elizabeth Fleming was waiting for her when she got back to the agency and Grace managed a tight smile.

'I don't think so,' she said, although in all honesty she had no idea what Jack had thought of the properties.

They'd walked back to their respective transport without speaking, and Grace had been only too happy to get behind the wheel of her car and drive away.

She'd been aware of him following her to the outskirts of town. But then, thankfully, he'd turned off, and she'd been so relieved to see him go that she hadn't considered the questions she might have to face when she got back to the agency.

In fact, as soon as his car had disappeared, she'd found a place to park and restored her hair to some semblance of order. It had been so much simpler to do that without him watching her, although her hands still trembled a little.

Her face hadn't been so easy to deal with. It wasn't difficult to spread a little hydrating make-up, or to add a trace of lip colour to her bare mouth.

But she couldn't disguise all the marks Jack's beard had left on her skin, or hide the swollen fullness of her lips.

'Are you all right?'

Clearly Elizabeth had noticed that she was avoiding her eyes, but there was no way Grace could confide in her. Dear God, she couldn't confide in anybody. And she was so angry with herself for behaving as she had.

Hadn't the experience she'd had with Sean been enough?

'I'm fine,' she said now, heading purposefully for her desk. 'But I've got to get in touch with Mrs Naughton. The window frames in those cottages are downright dangerous.'

'Are they?'

Elizabeth followed her to her desk, evidently waiting for an explanation.

Grace bent to stow her handbag in a drawer before straightening and saying briskly, 'You know the frames are rotten, don't you?'

'Well, I can imagine——' Elizabeth broke off

abruptly, gesturing towards Grace's jacket. 'Heavens, how did you do that?'

'Oh—'

Belatedly Grace remembered the stain she'd all but forgotten in her haste to restore other aspects of her appearance.

She smoothed a hand over her lapels. 'It was an accident.' She paused, and then, realising something more was needed, 'The gate stuck. I leant on it and *voila*! Instant ruin!'

'Dear me!' Elizabeth frowned. 'You must get the agency to pay your cleaning bill. If it will clean, of course.'

'I'm sure I can handle it,' averred Grace, not wanting any written reminder of that morning's fiasco.

In actual fact, she was thinking of dropping it into the next charity bag that came through the door. Anything to put the whole humiliating incident behind her.

'I suppose that's why you looked a bit upset when you came back,' remarked Elizabeth sympathetically, and to Grace's relief she turned away.

But then, almost immediately, she turned back again. 'Anyway, what were you saying about the cottage windows?'

'Oh—' Grace had hoped their conversation was over. But with the agency empty of any other clients at this moment, she was obliged to tell the other woman what Jack had said.

'I see.' Elizabeth nodded. 'Yes, that could be a

problem. You'd better ring Mrs Naughton and explain.' She grimaced. 'It's just possible it might persuade her to accept Grafton's offer, after all. She's an old woman. The last thing she needs is a potential lawsuit on her hands.'

Grace tended to agree, but the idea that William Grafton might get the cottages was still a tough pill to swallow.

Unfortunately, she was unable to get hold of Mrs Naughton that day. She'd speak to her the following day, even if it meant driving out to Mrs Naughton's house further along the coast. In fact, she thought she would enjoy that.

And it would get her out of the agency, just in case Jack decided to pay them another visit.

CHAPTER SIX

JACK WAS STILL in bed when his doorbell rang.

Muttering an oath, he buried his head under his pillow, trying to shut out the intrusive sound. He wasn't in the mood for visitors, and the uneasy suspicion that it could be Sean, come to seek retribution, wasn't something he wanted to deal with right now.

The doorbell rang again. More aggressively this time. The chimes echoed around the house like the peals of hell and he groaned before flinging back the covers and sliding his legs out of bed.

Then, uncaring that he was stark naked, he went to the window and peered out.

A car was parked at his gate. An unfamiliar car, whose long bonnet and angular lines spoke of another era. It was vintage, there was no doubt about that.

But who did it belong to?

Scowling, he turned back into the bedroom. The jeans he'd worn the night before were lying on a chair at the foot of his bed. Without bothering with any underwear, he pulled them on, snatching up a black tee as he opened the bedroom door.

By the time he'd negotiated the stairs, he was fairly decently dressed. Though his hair was probably sticking up in all directions and his feet were bare.

However, a burly individual, dressed in a double-breasted serge coat, stood on the path outside. The man, who was in his middle sixties, Jack guessed, was also wearing black breeches pushed into knee-high black boots, and for a moment Jack wondered if he'd stepped into an alternative universe.

The man started to introduce himself, but before he could do so an elderly lady emerged from the back of the vehicle.

'It's all right, James,' she said as he hurried to assist her. 'I can manage.' Beady brown eyes sought Jack's face as she brushed down the skirt of her fur-collared coat. 'Wait in the car, will you?'

'Yes, ma'am.'

James was evidently used to taking orders but he waited until his employer had reached the open doorway before getting back behind the wheel of the elderly limousine.

'Mr Connolly, I presume,' the woman said, looking up at Jack. 'I assume you're going to invite me in.'

Jack blew out a breath. 'Mrs Naughton?'

Who else could it be? From what he'd heard, the old lady lived in some style.

'I am.' She lifted artificially dark brows that had been expertly plucked to form a perfect arch. 'Well—may I come in?'

'Oh—yeah, sure.' Jack stepped back automatically, wincing at the chill of the hall floor beneath his feet. 'Come in.' He closed the door and gestured towards the living room. 'Can I get you some coffee?'

'Coffee!' The woman's voice was scornful as she crossed the hall and entered the living room. 'That's all you young people drink, isn't it? Don't you have any tea?'

'Yes, ma'am.' Jack found himself copying James's formality. 'I'll go and put the kettle on.'

Mrs Naughton glanced back at him. 'Don't you have a housekeeper, Mr Connolly?'

'Not today, ma'am.' Jack grimaced, aware that little in the room would escape her notice. 'Make yourself at home.'

In true 'watched pot' fashion, the kettle took for ever to boil. And by the time Jack had made a pot of tea for her and a mug of coffee for himself, fifteen minutes had passed.

He half expected Mrs Naughton to be examining the contents of his cupboards in his absence. But, in fact, she had seated herself in his favourite position by the window, apparently enjoying the view.

Jack set the tray on the low table beside her.

Then, seating himself on the wide windowsill, he said, 'Will you pour or shall I?'

If she was aware of the faint trace of mockery in his voice, she didn't show it.

'I'm not senile,' she said, pulling a face at his excuse for a milk jug. She viewed the milk residing in the small glass vase with a jaundiced eye. 'I trust this is clean.'

'As a whistle,' said Jack drily. 'You'll have to forgive my lack of tableware. I'm still discovering things I'm short of.'

Mrs Naughton snorted. 'And yet you want to take on more responsibilities,' she commented, lifting the teapot and filling her cup. 'Hmm, well, at least you make a decent pot of tea.'

Jack rubbed a hand over the stubble on his jaw. 'Even at nine o'clock in the morning,' he agreed drily.

Jack picked up his mug of coffee and swallowed a mouthful gratefully. Then, holding the cup between his palms, he said, 'So to what do I owe the honour of this visit?'

Mrs Naughton's brows arched again. 'You want to buy the cottages at Culworth, don't you?'

Jack's eyes widened now. 'Well, yes,' he said. Although he hadn't been into the agency again, he had spoken to the manager on the phone. 'But I understood from Mr Hughes that Mr Grafton had improved his offer.'

'He has. Marginally.' Mrs Naughton took a sip of her tea. 'But Grafton thinks he has me over a barrel because the cottages are in danger of collapsing.' She raised her cup again, regarding him shrewdly over the rim. 'I don't like being threatened, Mr Connolly.'

Jack frowned. 'The cottages are not in danger of collapsing,' he exclaimed impatiently. 'The insides need gutting, sure, but the walls seem solid enough.'

'That's what I said,' declared the old lady staunchly. 'I told Grant Hughes I'd had a surveyor take a look at them, and he was of the opinion that they were of no immediate danger to anyone.'

'Well, the window frames are crumbling,' offered Jack honestly.

He had no wish to bolster Grafton's claim, but it sounded as if Mrs Naughton's surveyor was saying what she wanted to hear.

'It looked as if there'd been kids squatting in one of the bedrooms,' he went on ruefully, despising himself for the sudden quickening of his pulse that that memory rekindled. 'The broken glass in the windows is a danger, too. But it shouldn't affect the value of the cottages themselves.'

'My sentiments exactly,' crowed the old lady, setting down her cup and watching Jack with triumphant eyes. 'That's why I've decided to give you the chance to make an offer. I've seen what you've done to this old place and I like the way you work.'

Jack shook his head, pushing all thoughts of Grace aside as he said, 'How did you know I was interested in the cottages?' There was no way Grace would have told her. 'Aren't you employing the agency to handle the sale for you?'

'I am.' Mrs Naughton was unperturbed. 'But Grant Hughes knows which way his bread's buttered, and I've put a lot of work the agency's way in recent years.'

Jack stared at her. 'So?'

'So—I asked him who it was looking around the cottages last week. He tried to put me off by saying that Ms Spencer didn't always consult him before showing a client round a piece of property, but he soon came round when I put a flea in his ear.'

Jack's lips twitched. The old lady was quite a character. But he'd already heard that from Grant Hughes himself.

'Anyway, I understand you were interested in the cottages, before Hughes stuck his oar in,' Mrs Naughton continued unabashed. 'And when I found out it was you, I thought I'd come and see for myself.'

Jack wasn't deceived. 'You'd like to see the house, wouldn't you?' he said flatly. 'Tell me, if you like what you see, do I get what I want?'

'Ah, I suppose that depends what you do want, Mr Connolly,' she replied cheerfully. 'I've checked up on you, you know, and it seems you're not short of a pound or two.'

Jack was amused. 'Do you vet all your prospective buyers?'

'No.' Mrs Naughton got to her feet to look down at him with critical eyes. 'But I'd hazard a guess that your interest was sparked by that foxy little lady who showed you round my property.' She laughed infectiously. 'Oh, yes, I have my spies, Mr Connolly. The church caretaker—who's retired now, of course—saw you pass his cottage. That's how I knew someone had been there.'

* * *

Grace heaved a sigh.

She really didn't want to work in the pub that evening. She had a thumping headache, and she'd been looking forward to having an early night.

She refused to accept that her headache had anything to do with the dressing-down she'd received from Mr Hughes that afternoon.

The agency manager had been at pains to tell her that Mrs Naughton had sold the Culworth cottages to Mr Connolly; the same Mr Connolly she'd escorted round the property over a week ago, without first getting permission from him.

To begin with, Grace had questioned his information.

To her knowledge—not to say her relief—Jack hadn't visited the agency again. She'd actually thought he blamed himself for what had happened and was doing her the courtesy of keeping away.

But no.

Mr Hughes had produced paperwork showing that Mr Connolly's legal representative was handling the sale for him. And what was more, he was furious with Grace for allowing it to happen.

'It won't do, you know,' he'd continued, his plump face flushed with irritation.

They'd been in the comparative privacy of his inner office, but Grace had had no doubt Elizabeth—and anyone else who was in the agency at this moment—could hear every word.

'Mr Grafton is a friend, and a long-time client of the agency. I know nothing about this Mr Connolly. Does he live in the area?'

Grace had been tempted to point out that if he studied the paperwork in front of him he could probably answer that question for himself.

'I believe he lives in Rothburn,' she'd told Mr Hughes and seen the way his face had contorted.

'You believe?' he'd said harshly. 'Do you deny that you're the reason Connolly learned about the Culworth cottages in the first place?'

'Yes!' Grace had been indignant. 'Yes, I do.' She'd licked her dry lips. 'I—I didn't mention the cottages to him. He just happened to be in the agency, talking to Elizabeth, and he overheard my conversation with Mr Grafton.'

She would have left it there, but it had been obvious Mr Hughes wasn't satisfied, so she'd continued. 'He's a friend of a friend, as a matter of fact. He and…someone I know were at university together.'

Mr Hughes had frowned. 'And now he just happens to live in this area?'

'Yes.'

The man's nostrils had flared. Clearly he hadn't liked that explanation any better, but, short of calling her a liar, there had been nothing he could do.

'Very well,' he'd said brusquely. 'But you'll have to tell Mr Grafton what's happened. He's your client. I suggest you have a word with him first thing in the morning.'

Which was not an interview Grace was looking forward to.

If she knew William Grafton, he'd not like the fact that he'd been outmanoeuvred over the cottages, and he would enjoy making her feel small.

'Grace! Gracie!'

Her father's voice floated up from the bottom of the stairs and Grace knew she couldn't delay any longer.

Swallowing a couple of aspirin with a mouthful of water from the bathroom tap, she surveyed her appearance without enthusiasm.

One of the reasons she was helping out behind the bar was because Rosie Phillips, her father's regular barmaid, had had to go to Newcastle to visit her ex-husband's mother, who was in the hospital there.

Still, she thought ruefully, as her headache began to recede, she might need this job if Mr Hughes decided to get rid of her.

She'd rifled her wardrobe for something appropriate to wear. But now the flimsy voile shirt worn over a jade-green vest looked rather showy for serving behind a bar.

Oh, well, she thought as her father shouted again, nothing ventured, nothing gained. Slipping her feet into wedges, she left the room and clattered down the stairs.

It was only seven o'clock and the bar was still fairly quiet. But there were glasses to dry and cases of soft drinks to stack behind the counter, and she was soon glad she hadn't worn something warmer. It might be a cool evening outside, but she was sweating.

She wasn't used to manual labour, she thought, recalling her life in London without regret. Maybe she could take up running again, now that she was living in Rothburn. For the past few years she'd had to content herself with an occasional trip to the gym.

The public bar got busier, and food orders started coming in, which meant that Grace had to divide her time between serving alcohol and delivering food, and her arms were soon aching. But at least her headache had virtually disappeared, which was a blessing.

She was carrying two plates of food through to the lounge bar when the swing doors that separated the outer and inner lobbies were pushed open.

A man came into the hall, his identity briefly disguised by the daylight streaming in behind him. A big man, tall and broad shouldered, who Grace had no difficulty in recognising as Jack Connolly.

He said he'd never visited the pub, she reminded herself, remembering Sean's comment about it being a small world with some annoyance.

Why had she remembered that? she wondered uneasily. It wasn't as if their conversation had been particularly memorable.

Unlike—

But she would not go there.

'Hi.'

Jack felt obliged to make the first overture. Though in all honesty, he was wondering if this had been such a bright idea.

Why had he felt the need to come and see Grace? Okay, the last time they'd been together, he hadn't exactly behaved honourably. And maybe he did owe her an apology for jumping on her as he had.

But, dammit, she hadn't exactly repulsed him. Someone should have told her that opening her mouth and tangling her tongue with his was not the way to turn him off.

'Hi,' Grace responded now, her voice slightly husky and unknowingly sensual to his ears. She nodded at the plates she was carrying. 'If you'll excuse me…'

'Wait!' Jack didn't know how else to say it. 'I'd like to talk to you.' He glanced about him. 'And I didn't know how else to get in touch with you out of office hours.'

'I don't think we have anything to talk about, Mr Connolly,' Grace murmured, using her back to push open the lounge bar door. 'Goodbye.'

Jack watched her disappear into the adjoining room with a feeling of frustration. He hadn't expected her to be pleased to see him, but did she have to be so damn offhand?

He scowled. The trouble was he hadn't been able to put what had happened out of his mind. He hadn't been able to think seriously about anything—or any-one—else since that morning at the cottage.

But that wasn't the only reason he was here, he reminded himself.

Getting that visit from Mrs Naughton a few days ago had definitely put him on the spot.

Of course, if he hadn't expected any comeback from the impulsive enquiry he'd had his solicitor make for him, he was naïve as well as stupid.

But he'd convinced himself that he had every right to make a bid for the cottages. The idea of develop-ing them, of using his skill and expertise to create a handful of desirable dwellings, had struck him as eminently sensible.

He needed something to do. Being a gentleman of leisure didn't really suit him. Okay, so he had no in-tention of getting his own hands dirty, but there was no reason why he shouldn't re-employ the tradesmen who'd made such a success of his house.

He pushed his thumbs into the front pockets of his jeans and considered his options. He could go into the bar and buy a drink and trust she was work-ing there, too.

Or he could just stay here and trust that there wasn't another exit from the lounge bar.

Apparently there wasn't.

Only a couple of minutes had elapsed before the door opened again and Grace reappeared.

She didn't seem surprised to find him still there,

but there was no trace of welcome in her expression, either.

Which was a pity, he reflected, because she looked pretty good otherwise. Apart from that first occasion at his house, he hadn't seen her in casual clothes. But the loose-fitting top over low-rise jeans really accentuated her shape and her femininity.

She would have walked past him, probably without saying anything, if Jack hadn't raised his hand to detain her.

But her response was predictable.

'Oh, please,' she said, making sure she remained well out of his reach. 'Isn't this getting rather old?' She sighed. 'Okay, perhaps I gave you the wrong impression that day at Culworth. But it was only a kiss, for goodness' sake!'

'I'm glad you see it that way.' Jack was unaccountably peeved, but he wasn't going to tell her that. He took a breath. 'If you must know, I came to apologise.'

'To apologise?'

Grace's voice squeaked and she silently berated herself for her inability to hide her feelings.

But, dammit, it was the last thing she'd expected him to say and she was momentarily robbed of speech.

'Yeah.' Jack rocked back on the heels of his boots. 'I know you hoped I'd given up on those cottages—'

Cottages? *Cottages?*

Grace blinked.

'—but I really think I can do some good with them.'

Grace's eyes widened.

How stupid could she be? He wasn't apologising for *kissing* her, for pity's sake. And, God, if she was honest, she'd admit that it had been so much more than a kiss. He was talking about the damn Culworth cottages.

She didn't speak and with a rueful little shrug Jack went on.

'I didn't honestly expect I'd get the opportunity to develop them. Not when Hughes told me Grafton had increased his offer. But Mrs Naughton said—'

That was too much.

'You contacted Mrs Naughton?' Grace exclaimed incredulously.

Oh, this just kept getting better and better. He'd actually gone behind Mr Hughes's back and spoken to Mrs Naughton personally. No wonder her boss had been so mad.

'No.' Jack blew out an aggravated breath. He knew exactly what she was thinking. 'She came to see me.'

Grace's jaw dropped. 'Mrs Naughton went to your house?' She put an unknowingly protective hand to her throat. 'I don't believe you.'

Yeah, he'd gathered that, and Jack was getting pretty annoyed by her attitude.

For God's sake, what was it with this woman?

Why did she persist in behaving as if he'd done something wrong?

Because whatever she says, you took advantage of her, his subconscious reminded him mildly, but he refused to listen.

'Well, whether you believe it or not, it's the truth,' he told her in a dangerously bland tone. 'People do come to my house, you know.' He paused. 'You did.'

Grace's lips tightened. 'How did she know where you lived?'

'I'm notorious.' Jack's tone was flat. 'I thought you knew that.'

Grace's face suffused with colour.

Once again, her feelings had betrayed her. And it didn't help that she knew her overreaction had more to do with her own unwilling awareness of the man than with any legitimate grievance she might have over the cottages.

'I have to go,' she said, aware that she'd said that before, too.

But she had spent considerably longer than she should have done arguing with Jack, when her father was working, single-handed, behind the bar.

'Okay.'

Jack lifted his shoulders in a dismissive gesture, and she wished she weren't so hung up on the lean male strength of his body.

But in tight jeans that moulded every muscle and a plum-coloured tee with buttons that were open at his throat, he was undeniably good to look at.

And she was looking, she realised, hurriedly pulling her eyes away.

But he'd noticed.

'Don't beat yourself up,' he said, his voice low and disturbingly attractive. 'You can tell Sean it was all my fault, and if he wants to beat me up—'

Grace gasped. 'Sean doesn't beat people up,' she said tersely.

Particularly not if he thought he'd get the worst of it.

'Doesn't he?' Jack's reaction was enigmatic. 'No? Well, perhaps he should.'

Would that have made you feel better? Grace wondered, annoyed because she knew what had happened had been as much her fault as Jack's.

'He's not an animal,' she said primly, ignoring her conscience. 'I assume you're saying that if Lisa had been unfaithful, that's what you'd have done.'

'Unfaithful!'

Jack was incensed by her attitude. And by her ability to catch him on the raw. The truth was, he hadn't even thought of Lisa when he'd been kissing Grace.

And that was the most infuriating thing of all.

Whatever he might have said next was baulked, however. The swing doors behind him opened and two men came into the lobby.

They were strangers to Grace, but she could tell from the glances that passed between them that they thought they were interrupting a private conversation.

Or a lovers' meeting, she thought uneasily as the two men shouldered their way into the bar.

'I really have to go,' she said again, aware that in some subtle way the situation had changed.

'Be my guest.'

Jack pushed his hands into the back pockets of his jeans, making no further attempt to detain her.

Perhaps because he was tempted to do just that, he thought irritably as she put her hand on the door the two men had just passed through.

Grace hesitated then. She was prone to do that, he'd noticed.

'You—you're not staying for a drink?'

Jack gave her a speaking look. 'You're surprised?'

'Well—it's a public bar,' she muttered defensively. 'I can't stop you.'

'No.' Jack acknowledged the admission, his eyes dark and impenetrable behind the fringe of his lashes. 'But you don't want me here. And I do have some feelings, you know.'

'And if I said I don't mind what you do?'

'I'd say that was pretty obvious,' retorted Jack drily. 'Thanks for the offer, Grace, but no, thanks.'

'Grace!'

Grace recoiled as the door to the bar was propelled open in spite of her resistance.

'Dad!' she exclaimed, half in dismay, half in protest. 'You nearly knocked me over.'

Mr Spencer didn't immediately say anything.

But his eyes moved instinctively towards her companion.

And Jack, who hadn't had the chance to make his escape, thought that, judging by the older man's expression, he and Grace must look as guilty as he felt.

CHAPTER SEVEN

'IS SOMETHING WRONG, GRACE?'

Mr Spencer's tone was more curious than un-friendly and Jack watched the way Grace's tongue moved over her parted lips.

But for once the provocation that evoked was overwhelmed by his need to explain who he was.

'I'm Jack Connolly, Mr Spencer,' he said. 'I was just telling Grace about an offer I've made on some property the agency was dealing with.'

He grinned, and Grace despised herself for think-ing how disarming—and disreputable, she reminded herself—he could be.

'I'm sure she was bored silly,' Jack was going on charmingly. 'And I should have known better than to expect her to discuss business matters out of of-fice hours.'

'Well, Grace is working for me at the moment,' Mr Spencer remarked drily.

He turned to his daughter. 'Will's got at least four meals waiting for you to serve.'

'I'll get to it.'

Grace forced a half-rueful smile in Jack's direc-tion before heading into the bar. She thought her fa-ther forgot sometimes that she wasn't the schoolgirl she'd been before she left for university. But he'd always been keen to vet any boyfriend she'd brought to the pub.

Not that Jack Connolly was a boyfriend, she reminded herself impatiently. And her father hadn't shown any more sense than she had where Sean Nesbitt was concerned.

Left alone, the two men eyed one another with enforced politeness.

'I'm afraid my daughter doesn't really care for working in the bar,' Mr Spencer declared pleasantly, more relaxed now that his customers' needs were being seen to. 'I'm Tom Spencer, Grace's father, of course. Have we met?'

'I'm afraid not. I only moved into the village about eighteen months ago,' explained Jack at once. 'I've been renovating that old property on the coast road.'

'Really?'

Despite his words, Jack had the feeling Tom Spencer had known who he was all along.

'You know my daughter's boyfriend, I believe.'

'That's right.'

'Sean.' Tom Spencer nodded. 'He's a good chap, Sean. My wife and I are very fond of him.'

Just in case you have any doubts about that, thought Jack drily.

'Anyway, how is the renovation going, Mr Connolly?'

'Jack,' said Jack politely. 'I finished a couple of months ago. Lindisfarne House has been quite an undertaking.' He wasn't quite sure where this was going. 'But I enjoyed it.'

'I'm sure.'

Tom Spencer considered for a moment and then he gestured towards the bar.

'You must come in and let me buy you a drink,' he said after a moment. 'We always welcome newcomers into the pub.'

'Oh, I don't think—'

Jack started to protest but Tom Spencer was adamant.

'It's the least I can do after interrupting your conversation with Grace.' He pushed open the door of the bar and stood back invitingly. 'I'm interested to hear about this new property you're hoping to buy.'

Ah! Jack was cynical. He had the feeling Spencer didn't want to encourage his association with his daughter, but he was not above hearing a little gossip himself.

But it would have been rude to refuse. So with a slight shrug of his shoulders, he preceded the man into the warm alcohol-laden atmosphere of the bar.

There was no sign of Grace. She had obviously gone to collect the meals waiting to be delivered. And sure enough, she emerged through a swing door a few moments later carrying a tray on which resided four plates of food.

The only sign that she was surprised to see Jack was the way her eyes widened before darting curiously towards her father.

She was probably wondering what they'd been talking about, Jack reflected half irritably. Did she honestly think her father would be making nice with him if he'd told him about their visit to Culworth?

At Tom Spencer's suggestion, he took a seat at the bar and ordered a pint of beer. He would have preferred a bottle, but the beer when it came was good; rich and creamy, its head smearing his upper lip with foam.

However, before her father could start asking him about the property he was interested in and what he planned to do with it, Grace was back.

She slipped behind the bar, successfully manoeuvring Tom Spencer into a position where he was obliged to serve a waiting customer. Then she snatched up a cloth to wipe the bar in front of Jack.

'You changed your mind,' she said, and Jack couldn't tell whether she was glad or sorry. She glanced sideways at her father. 'I hope Dad's not been giving you a hard time.'

'I can handle it.' Jack took another mouthful of his beer and wiped his mouth on the back of his hand. 'How about you?'

'What about me?'

Grace looked up at him in alarm, and Jack was struck once again by the clear transparency of those green eyes. He wanted to reach out, to cup her anxious face in his hands and smooth the darkness beneath her eyes with his thumbs.

There was a pulse beating urgently in her temple and he knew he'd find a matching palpitation beneath her ear. Silky strands of red-gold hair had escaped from the knot on top of her head, and he wanted to sweep them aside and taste the slight dampness of her skin with his tongue.

And knew he couldn't answer her question.

Not without betraying feelings he had no desire to put on display. He shouldn't have come here; he shouldn't have accepted her father's invitation.

But, most of all, he so shouldn't have sampled something that was proving to be so damned addictive.

He took another generous swallow of his drink and put his almost-empty glass down on the bar.

Grace glanced at it and then said impulsively, 'Let me get you another beer.'

"No, one's enough,' he assured her easily. 'It was good. Thank your dad for me, won't you?'

'You're leaving?'

'Isn't that what you want?'

Grace blew out a breath.

It had been. It should still be, she knew. Because whatever attraction Jack Connolly might have for her, it was just a fleeting thing.

He must have loved his wife once, and, although it might be too late to regard his behaviour towards her as a rebound, he wasn't seriously interested in her, either.

Nor she in him.

'I—I was going to ask you what Mrs Naughton

had said,' she lied, having just thought of that on the spur of the moment. 'What did you think of her? She's quite a character, isn't she?'

'Quite a character,' agreed Jack drily. 'Do you know her?'

'Only slightly.' Grace took a moment to serve another customer and then came back. 'It was me who handled her initial inquiry about selling the cottages.'

'Yeah, I guessed that. To Grafton.'

Grace grimaced. 'I have to tell him the cottages have been sold to someone else tomorrow. He's not going to be pleased.'

And wasn't that an understatement?

Jack frowned. 'Would you like me to do it for you?'

It was certainly a temptation, but Grace shook her head. 'It's my job. Mr Hughes was very definite about that.'

'Hughes? Oh, he's the guy in the agency.'

'My boss, in other words.'

Grace gave him a mischievous grin. Really, she thought, she enjoyed talking to Jack when there were no sexual undercurrents in his conversation. Although, if she was honest, she would admit she didn't exactly dislike them, either.

He was different from Sean. For one thing, his eyes weren't constantly moving round the bar, checking out the other talent. He actually seemed interested in what she was saying, and she wished desperately that Sean's problems weren't still ruling her life.

She moved to attend another customer and when she came back, Jack slid off his stool. 'Hey, I can see you're busy,' he said, wondering if it was only his imagination that made him think the atmosphere between them had changed. 'Don't forget to thank your father for the beer.' He stepped away, uneasily aware that he had forgotten all about Sean for the past half hour. And that wouldn't do. 'Goodnight, Grace.'

Grace knew that her farewell was less than enthusiastic. Dear God, she hadn't wanted him to go. But she was obliged to serve a man who'd come to refill an order and by the time that was done, Jack was long gone.

Almost at once, her father came to join her. 'Mr Connolly's left?' he remarked inquiringly. 'What was he saying to you?'

'This and that.' Grace wasn't in the mood to be tactful. 'We were talking about the cottages. What else?'

'I'm only curious. You seemed very…friendly.'

'Oh, Dad!'

'Does Sean know him well? I'd have my suspicions about him, if I was your boyfriend.'

'Sean's not my boyfriend any more, Dad!' She sighed. Why had she said that?

'I know he still cares about you,' retorted her father impatiently. 'All young couples have rows. But they get over them.'

'Maybe.' If only there was some way she could get her parents' money back. Then she wouldn't have to pretend any longer. 'In any case, Jack Connolly is not interested in me.'

'You don't think so?'

'He's a client, Dad. I may be helping you out here, but the agency is my job.'

Tom Spencer frowned. 'He's your client? You're the one who's dealing with his offer?'

'Well, no.' Grace was already regretting saying as much as she had. Any minute now, her father was going to remind her that William Grafton was a friend. 'But—I did show him the property last week.'

'Hmm.' Her father didn't sound too happy. 'So, you'll know what he plans to do with the property?'

'Yes.'

'Well, go on.'

'Dad, I hardly know Jack Connolly. I believe he's an architect. He probably plans to develop the cottages in much the same way as Mr Grafton.'

'So how come he got the cottages? Wasn't Will first in line?'

'Will? Oh, you mean Mr Grafton. Well, he was, but Mrs Naughton decided she preferred Mr Connolly's offer. It's not my fault. She can sell them to whoever she likes!'

It was getting dark by the time Jack got back to Lindisfarne House. And, when he opened the door and stepped into the hall, he knew instantly he wasn't alone.

When he switched on the lights, he saw Lisa sitting halfway up the stairs, legs crossed, her single sandal balanced precariously on one swinging foot, her silver cap of hair gleaming ethereally in the glow from the chandelier above her head. 'I thought you never went into public houses.'

'Never is a long time,' retorted Jack shortly, and, without waiting for her response, he strode purposefully into the kitchen.

He'd had no dinner, but he wasn't hungry. Nevertheless, he filled the coffee filter and switched it on. He felt aggressive and not a little edgy. And it wasn't Lisa's appearance that was steering his mood.

'There's a casserole in the fridge.' Lisa had come to stand in the open doorway. 'Mrs Honeyman brought it with her this morning.'

Mrs Honeyman was the housekeeper. And, because she worried that he wasn't eating properly on his own, she often left some tasty dish she'd made herself in his fridge.

Jack grunted, but he merely reached for a mug and slammed it down onto the granite counter.

He felt like warning Lisa that he wasn't in the mood for small talk. But he knew from past experience she'd only go when she'd said what she had to say.

'What's got you in such a foul mood?' she persisted, and Jack regarded her with baleful eyes.

'Not your business,' he said tersely. 'And unless you're looking for a fight, I suggest you stay out of my way.'

'Ooh!' Lisa's thin brows rose in mock alarm. 'I'm scared.'

Jack didn't answer her. He was seriously peeved and talking to a ghost simply wasn't going to cut it.

'I gather you've had another run-in with the delicious Ms Spencer.'

Lisa had never known when to keep her mouth shut and Jack gave her a weary look.

'Get lost, Lisa.'

'I was afraid she might be trouble,' she murmured ruefully. 'And I'm not particularly flattered that you can blow me off without a thought.'

'Yeah, right.'

'I mean it.' She was indignant now. 'I've got used to you being on your own.'

Jack scowled. 'Hey, don't look now, but I am on my own,' he stated flatly. 'She has a boyfriend. Remember?'

'Sean Nesbitt!' Lisa spoke scathingly. 'Yeah, well, I shouldn't let that trouble you.'

'What do you mean?'

Jack stared at her, but she was already fading. 'Oh, nothing,' she said, lifting her shoulders in a dismissive gesture.

And just like that, she was gone.

Jack swore his frustration. Pouring himself a mug

of strong black coffee, he took a reckless mouthful, almost scalding his mouth in the process.

He was seriously losing it, he thought bitterly. How much longer was he going to go on talking to a ghost? It was just as well he'd found himself an occupation. At least it would get him out of the house.

Three weeks later, he signed the papers that made the Culworth cottages his.

Despite a warning from his surveyor that there could be structural problems down the line, Jack had had the solicitor who'd handled his purchase of Lindisfarne House deal with the legal jargon.

And, in consequence, the sale had gone through without a hitch. Mrs Naughton had been pleased. She'd actually invited Jack to have dinner with her one evening—an invitation he'd not as yet taken her up on.

The agency had been less enthusiastic.

Although Mrs Naughton had paid the agency their commission, on the one occasion Jack had had to go in and see Grant Hughes, he'd been less than impressed.

In his opinion, Grace's boss was an ignorant oaf, whose resentment stemmed more from the fact that she had actually initiated a sale that he'd earmarked for one of his cronies, than from the fact that Mrs Naughton had chosen to interfere in the process.

Jack had wondered if he'd see Grace when he went into the agency. But he hadn't.

Only Mrs Fleming had occupied one of the two desks in the outer office. And although Jack had been tempted to ask where the other girl was, he'd restrained himself.

In fact, he'd come to the conclusion that he was unlikely to see her again. Which was just as well, he told himself.

Then, on Saturday morning, Jack had an unpleasant surprise.

He'd come home after spending the morning out at Culworth with his builder. And once again, he wasn't dressed to receive visitors.

So when he saw the silver Mercedes parked at his gate, his heart sank.

The car was empty, however, and, thrusting open the door of the Lexus, Jack got out and looked around.

There was no one about, and he breathed a sigh of relief, wondering if the Mercedes could conceivably belong to someone else.

Deciding it wasn't his problem, he hauled his jacket out of the back of the Lexus. Then, stepping up to his door, he juggled his keys until he found the right one and inserted it in the lock.

He was looking forward to the shower he'd been promising himself since a wall in one of the cottage bedrooms had collapsed. He and his companion had been covered with brick dust and he could feel it still in the gritty scrape of his scalp.

He couldn't wait to get his clothes off and he was

already pulling his sweatshirt over his head as he stepped over the threshold.

'Hey, Jack! Jack, hold up.'

The voice was unmistakeable and Jack fisted the offending sweatshirt even as Sean—and Grace—appeared from around the back of the building.

He was intensely aware that he was sweating. That rivulets of perspiration were moistening the hair between his nipples, and the hair at the nape of his neck.

'We were just admiring your garden,' Sean exclaimed cheerfully, not at all perturbed at being caught out. 'Weren't we, Grace? We guessed—or rather, we hoped—you'd be back for lunch.'

Grace managed a resigned smile of acknowledgement. But her nerves were jumping at the sight of Jack standing, bare-chested, in the doorway.

If she'd thought he'd looked good in a tee shirt, he looked infinitely more disturbing without it. A broad chest, liberally spiked with dark hair, tapered down to a flat stomach, ribbed with muscle.

Faded jeans hung precariously from lean hips and she guessed if they'd been a few minutes later the jeans would have been discarded, as well.

Did he wear underwear? she wondered, feeling her breathing quicken at the images this thought evoked. Probably not, she decided a little grudgingly.

'Well…' Jack stepped back from the door, aware that he was obliged to invite them in. 'Come in.' He gestured towards the living room. 'You know the way. Just give me a minute, will you? I need to freshen up.'

'That you do, old buddy,' said Sean pointedly, touching his nose with a delicate finger, and Grace wanted to slap him.

The scent of Jack's skin got to her, too, but she didn't find it at all offensive. On the contrary, it caused her own skin to prickle with unwanted awareness. And, feeling the sudden dampness between her legs, she was glad she wasn't wearing jeans.

'Okay.' Jack's eyes connected with Grace's for a moment. But his belated, 'Hi, Grace. Nice to see you again,' was in sharp contrast to the heat that was emanating from his body.

It was as if any personal contact between them had been erased from his memory. And she sucked in a nervous little breath before preceding Sean into the attractive living room they'd seen before.

CHAPTER EIGHT

TOLD YOU, SEAN MOUTHED as soon as they heard Jack vaulting up the stairs. 'I knew he'd be about here somewhere.'

Grace shrugged. 'He could have been over at Culworth. In fact, I think that's where he has been,' Grace averred, eager to keep their conversation impersonal. 'You must have seen the way his hair was coated with grit. It looked as if he'd been working on the cottages himself.'

Which was so not something she wanted to think about.

'Who cares?' Sean spoke carelessly. He dropped down onto a squashy leather sofa and patted the seat beside him. 'Come here. I want to tell you how grateful I am that you agreed to come here with me. It's been ages since you've talked to me. I'm still hoping you might change your mind about staying up here.'

'I'm not just "staying up here", am I, Sean?' Grace exclaimed irritably, making quotation marks with her fingers to emphasise her point. 'And I'm only here because Dad insisted I couldn't let you come on your own.'

In fact, her father was still suspicious about Jack Connolly's visit to the pub to see her. And the last thing she needed was her dad bringing that up in front of Sean.

Nevertheless, she had been taken aback when Sean had walked into the pub the previous evening. It was seven weeks since he'd returned to London, and she'd half hoped he'd got the message as far as she was concerned. It did cross her mind—hopefully—that he might have some good news as far as finding an investor for his website was concerned. Did he ever intend to pay her father back?

But nothing with Sean was that easy.

However, according to what he'd told her father, he had been busy 'networking'. Grace had no idea how true that was but she'd clutch at any straw in the present situation.

That there'd been no takers was perfectly obvious. And he hadn't been too pleased, either, when Mr Spencer had had to tell him he couldn't stay at the Bay Horse.

A surfing competition was taking place just along the coast and, because they hadn't known he was coming, the pub's two spare rooms had been taken.

Sean had had the sense not to suggest that he share Grace's room. The answer would have been no, of course, and he'd known that. Instead, he'd accepted their suggestion that he stay at a local bed and breakfast down the road.

The trouble was Grace suspected she knew why Sean was here. He'd had no success raising funds in London and she was fairly sure he intended to hit on Jack for a loan.

And while the idea might make her cringe, she couldn't deny the slender hope that Jack might be the way out of her difficulties. She despised herself for even thinking it, but was it possible that Jack's money might save the pub?

Conversely, Jack didn't strike her as the kind of man to be taken in so easily. It was just another website, for goodness' sake. And there were dozens of comparison sites out there already. Sean's idea was not that original. She could only hope and pray that somehow a miracle might happen.

'Come on.' Sean's tone was wheedling now. 'At least pretend we're still a couple. Don't embarrass me in front of Jack.'

Embarrass *him*?

Grace closed her eyes against the images that suddenly assaulted her senses. Was it really better to pretend she supported Sean than to admit she was afraid of her feelings for Jack?

Grace was still thinking about this when Sean got impatiently to his feet.

'Hey, do you think Jack would mind if I helped myself to a beer?' He was tense and nervy, probably apprehensive about what he was going to say. 'I'm thirsty.'

'You can't go poking around in someone else's kitchen,' Grace protested. She pointed to the window, drawing his attention in that direction. 'Look at that fantastic view! I wonder if the surfing competition has started yet. It might be interesting to watch.'

'Are you kidding me?' Sean was contemptuous. 'If you think I want to waste my time watching a bunch of muscleheads in wetsuits, trying to stay upright on an ironing board, you're very much mistaken.'

'It wasn't an invitation,' retorted Grace tightly, and then she caught her breath when Jack spoke behind them.

'I think it's a bit more demanding than that,' he remarked, and they both swung round—Grace almost guiltily—to find their host standing in the doorway.

He'd evidently had a swift shower and Grace could see drops of water glistening on his shaggy dark hair. He looked unbearably masculine and so sexy she felt every nerve in her body go on high alert.

In low-waisted khakis that hugged his narrow hips and a black collarless body shirt, he exuded a raw sensual appeal that she'd never experienced before meeting him. And the fact that his body hadn't been completely dry when he'd got dressed meant that the cotton fabrics clung to him in all the most disturbing places.

Thankfully, Sean had his own agenda.

'Jack, my man,' he exclaimed expansively, leaving Grace and turning to Jack. 'We were just admiring your view.'

'Were you?'

Jack's dry comment made Grace almost sure he'd heard every word Sean had said.

'Yeah.' Sean was undaunted. 'So, how are you, Jack? Still living the life of a beachcomber?'

'Don't you mean a beach bum?' suggested Jack, undeterred, and Sean had the grace to pull a wry face.

'Whatever,' he muttered. He thrust his hands into the back pockets of his chinos and pushed his chest out. 'Anyway, how about offering me a beer? Trailing around your garden is thirsty work.'

'Okay.'

Jack half turned away. Then he looked back, straight at Grace.

'What would you like?'

How to answer that?

Grace felt the treacherous colour rising up her face at the thoughts she couldn't quite keep at bay.

Jack, naked, in her bed, was in there somewhere. As was the compelling prospect of repeating that kiss that had purely blown her mind.

She shivered. How pathetic was that? He could seduce her brain with only a look.

'Um—anything,' she mumbled, aware that Sean was looking at her now.

'So long as it's not beer, eh, Grace?' he said mockingly, and she struggled to find a smile.

Jack's dark brows arched. 'White wine?'

'Fine,' she said. 'That would be nice.'

'I'll come with you.'

Without waiting for an invitation, Sean followed Jack out of the room and Grace sank down rather weakly onto the nearest chair. Right now, it was hard to care what Sean intended. So long as her unwanted attraction to Jack wasn't exposed.

Jack entered his kitchen with Sean behind him.

He was a bit aggrieved at the other man's presumption, but he tamped it down. Remembering the way he'd betrayed their friendship was a rude wake-up call.

Jack pulled open the fridge door, taking out two beers and a bottle of Chardonnay. He handed one of the beers to Sean and then jerked open a drawer, looking for the corkscrew. 'Do you need a glass?'

'Nuh-uh.' Sean borrowed the corkscrew to hook off the cap of his beer, then perched himself on one of the tall stools that faced a central island, surveying the copper pans hanging from the units, the bowls of climbing plants and pots of herbs suspended from the beamed ceiling.

'This is some place,' he said, taking a long drink of his beer. 'I bet it cost a small fortune.'

'Actually, I got it fairly reasonably,' said Jack, despite his dislike of discussing money. 'As Grace's father has probably told you, it was in pretty dire straits when I took it over.'

'Ah, but you didn't do all this,' said Sean, gesturing with his bottle. 'I mean, come on, Jack. You're no do-it-yourselfer, are you?'

'You'd be surprised.' Jack had no intention of telling Sean exactly what he had done during the course of the renovation. 'How about you? Have you found a post in Northumberland, or have you decided to stay in London?'

Sean shrugged. 'As a matter of fact, I haven't been looking. But don't tell Grace that. I'm still hoping to find a backer for my website.' He swallowed the remainder of his beer. 'Got any ideas?'

Jack frowned. 'Do you need a backer to start a website? I'd have thought it was a fairly simple thing to arrange.'

'Not the kind of website I have in mind,' Sean contradicted him shortly. Then he held up his empty bottle. 'You got another one of these?'

'Sure.'

Jack opened the fridge again and handed him another beer. Then he said pointedly, 'Oughtn't we to be getting back to Grace? She'll be wondering where we are.'

'Oh, Grace is okay.' Sean opened his bottle and took another generous swig. 'Man, that really hits the spot.'

Jack said nothing and after a moment, Sean met his gaze.

'Why don't you tell me what you think of her. Grace, I mean.' There was a sly shrewdness to the question. 'You've seen her, haven't you? Since I went back to London.'

Jack kept his reaction securely under control. 'I

assume you mean at the agency,' he said neutrally. 'Yes. She showed me the cottages at Culworth.'

'Mmm.' Sean's eyes narrowed. 'So go on. What do you think of her?' His mouth twisted. 'You can tell me.'

Jack could feel a simmering sense of resentment stirring inside him. Where the hell was Sean going with a question like that?

'What do you want me to say?' he asked, restraining his temper with an effort. 'She seems very nice. Very efficient.' The words almost stuck in his throat. 'You're a very lucky man.'

'Yeah, I am, aren't I?' Sean took a moment to enjoy the compliment. 'But she deserves so much more than I can give her.' He grimaced. 'Ever since I lost that job with Sunyata, it's been a struggle to make ends meet.'

Jack suspected that was an exaggeration. Sean's job and the salary Grace had earned as a paralegal would have surely added up to quite a comfortable income.

'Anyway…' Sean wasn't finished '…we all know it's okay for you, Jack. You don't have to go bowing and scraping for every penny you need.'

'Nor do you,' said Jack mildly, but now Sean's jaw jutted aggressively.

'I do, if I want to make anything of myself,' he exclaimed harshly. 'I don't have a wealthy grandmother to help me out.'

Jack sighed. 'I'm sorry you feel like that, Sean,' he said. 'But I haven't had it all my own way.'

Sean's mouth thinned. 'You mean, because of Lisa.'

'Yeah, because of Lisa,' Jack agreed, feeling another twinge of guilt at the realisation that he hadn't thought about his wife in days.

Grace, yes. God help him, he'd thought about her a lot. Because despite his conscious determination to stay well away from her, he couldn't control his subconscious so easily.

Which, let's face it, he thought, was why he was letting Sean Nesbitt pull his strings.

Sean shrugged. 'Lisa was a beautiful woman,' he conceded, though there was little real sympathy in his voice. 'And I know you loved her.' He paused. 'But you have to admit, she was no saint.'

Jack scowled. 'What's that supposed to mean?'

As far as he was aware, Sean had met Lisa only a couple of times; one of them at their wedding. Certainly not enough to pass judgement on her character.

'I'm only saying, it's a couple of years since the accident,' Sean muttered offhandedly. 'And your life has had its compensations, if you know what I mean.'

'Okay.' Jack had had enough of this. 'If you've got something to say, why don't you spit it out?'

Sean hunched his shoulders. 'You always were an arrogant bastard, weren't you?'

'And you know damn well you're only here because you need my help.'

'All right, all right.' Sean pulled a face 'I'll tell you about my idea for a website.' He paused for a moment and then added confidently, 'It's a comparison site. And I know there are lots of them. But this is like nothing you've seen before.'

It was fully half an hour before the two men returned to the living room.

Grace had pulled a sailing magazine off the coffee table and was flicking through the pages in an effort to ignore what she was sure was going on in the other room.

Sean hadn't gone with Jack because he wanted to check out his kitchen. He'd seen an opportunity to speak to him without her obvious disapproval and jumped at it.

Sean's face as he came back into the room mirrored a smug satisfaction. Grace felt her stomach tighten at the realisation that he must have achieved his objective.

But how had he achieved it? Why had Jack succumbed so easily? Was it because he saw some merit in his website idea? Or because he felt guilty after that torrid embrace in the cottage at Culworth?

She suspected the latter, particularly as Jack's expression was decidedly cynical. It irritated her beyond measure that Sean had put them in such a position and she wished she could just leave him to it.

'White wine?'

Jack was offering her a glass and she was obliged to take it.

But she deliberately avoided his eyes as she did so. Even if she couldn't prevent the little frisson of electricity that shot up her arm when his fingers touched hers.

'Thanks,' she muttered a little ungraciously and felt even worse when Sean came to perch on the arm of her chair.

'Guess what?' he said, and she wondered if he really believed she didn't know exactly what he was going to say.

'What?' she asked dutifully, aware that once again Jack had chosen to remain on his feet, propped against the small bureau at the other side of the room.

He still wasn't wearing any shoes, she noticed out of the corner of her eye. And despised herself for finding the omission unbearably sexy.

But what was new? she asked herself resignedly. Everything about Jack Connolly was sexy, and for some reason her body refused to ignore the fact.

'Jack's agreed to look at my idea,' Sean declared, with a self-satisfied smile. 'I told you he'd be interested. He's like me. He knows a good investment when he sees one.'

Grace had to bite back the words that Jack was nothing like Sean. But that didn't make them any less true, and she felt a weary sense of depression digging at her temples.

Why couldn't Sean have waited until he'd saved enough money for him to speculate on something as risky as this on his own? He'd already almost bankrupted her parents with his lies. And he must know that for every website that succeeded, at least a dozen others failed.

'Well?' Sean knew she resented him sitting on the arm of her chair but he seemed indifferent to her feelings. 'Don't you have anything to say? Aren't you going to congratulate me on being such an astute salesman?'

Grace's lips felt frozen.

She knew she had to say something. But she made the mistake of looking up instead. And the contempt in Jack's brooding countenance was like a chill finger down her spine.

'Um—that's wonderful news,' she managed at last. What else could she say, in the circumstances? And, although it sounded unconvincing to her own ears, Sean evidently only heard what he wanted to hear.

Jack pushed himself up from the bureau and looked away before he said something he'd regret.

But, dammit, it was bad enough having to watch that oaf with Grace without hearing her endorse her boyfriend's sordid little game.

To his relief, Sean seemed to realise he should quit while he was ahead. Getting up from the chair, he said, 'I guess we should be going. Grace's mother worries and we have been out rather longer than we expected.'

Grace bit her tongue until it bled.

Sean had never given a damn about her mother's feelings before.

But perhaps he could see that Jack had evidently had enough of them. Even Sean's thick skin must have some sensitivity, after all.

CHAPTER NINE

'YOU'RE NOT SERIOUSLY going into business with Sean Nesbitt!'

It was the following morning, and, after a restless night plagued with dreams of Grace and Sean together, Jack had decided to make himself a bacon sandwich.

'What's it to you?' Jack demanded, casting a dour glance in Lisa's direction. 'It's not as if you're going to lose anything by it.'

Lisa made a sound of protest. 'I'm hurt,' she exclaimed, lowering her shoeless foot to the floor. She was standing at the other side of the island, arms crossed and ready for a fight.

'I know the feeling,' Jack said now, forking crisp slices of bacon onto a wedge of wholemeal bread. He shrugged. 'But he's right. I have been lucky. Financially, anyway. And maybe I do owe him something for all the years we were good pals.'

Lisa snorted. 'Sean Nesbitt was never a "good pal" of yours,' she retorted shortly.

Then she stifled a groan. 'Uh-oh! Here comes trouble!'

'What do you mean?'

Jack lifted his head to look at her just as Lisa's image began to fade. Instead, he saw Mrs Honeyman through the kitchen window—at least half an hour early, by his estimation—cycling into the yard at the side of the house.

He swore roundly, understanding perfectly what Lisa had meant.

But then he crossed the stone tiles to unlatch the outer door with a certain resignation. Mrs Honeyman always came into the house through the old boot room, changing from her outdoor shoes into the soft-soled trainers in which she preferred to work.

'Mr Connolly!'

Her first words needed no further explanation and Jack sighed.

'Yeah, I know,' he said, 'Fried food is bad for my digestion. But I was hungry!'

Mrs Honeyman merely shook her head and began clearing up the mess he'd made. The frying pan went into soapy water; the utensils he'd used were rinsed and put into the dishwasher. Then, after eyeing Jack, munching on his sandwich, she said, 'I assume you'd like some coffee with that?'

Jack's mouth was full, but he nodded his approval, deciding not to tell her he'd had at least three mugs of his favourite brew already.

A sturdy woman, in her middle fifties, Mrs Honeyman had been the first person to answer Jack's advertisement for a part-time housekeeper. And she and Jack had hit it off at once, making any other interviews he'd conducted superfluous.

Of course, she occasionally despaired of his eating habits. Usually, it had to be said, because she deplored his practice of buying fast food. But in the past few weeks, her attitude had turned to one of concern.

'As I'll be here all day, would you like me to make you some lunch?' she suggested. 'I've got some nice fresh tomatoes in my bag, and I could mince the remains of the steak I used yesterday and make you a dish of bolognese.'

Jack blew out a breath.

'Well, that's very kind of you, Mrs Honeyman—'

'But?'

'—but I won't be in for lunch,' he said apologetically. 'I'm meeting the builder at Culworth, and I'll probably have a sandwich with him!'

'Another sandwich!'

Mrs Honeyman raised her eyebrows, and Jack gave her a rueful smile. He could have told her that while the renovations were going on he'd eaten anything he could lay his hands on. And that included days-old sandwiches whose sell-by date was long past.

'Anyway,' she went on, 'don't you worry. I'll see that you have some fresh vegetables for your dinner. And maybe a fresh steak pie to go with them.'

Jack shook his head. 'You spoil me, Mrs. Honeyman.'

'Well, somebody has to,' she declared. 'It's time you thought about getting yourself a lady friend.

Respecting your late wife is all well and good, but a man needs a woman in his—'

She broke off abruptly, her cheeks flushing again, and Jack decided to put her out of her misery.

'Yeah, I know what you mean,' he said ruefully, aware that Mrs Honeyman didn't know how inspired her words had been.

He'd had a woman in his bed last night. Unfortunately, the woman in question had known nothing about it.

Grace drove the last half mile to the church and pulled in behind a battered pickup.

The small parking area was busy, she saw, with a smart little Audi and a more sedate Honda filling the space. But there was no sign of the expensive Lexus SUV and Grace's heart sank.

She'd been so sure she'd find Jack here.

According to what she'd heard in the agency— though no one had actually discussed the matter with her, of course—planning permission for the cottages had been granted without a hitch. With Mrs Naughton's active participation, the whole deal had been accomplished in a little over three weeks.

Of course, Grace reflected now, there was no real reason why Jack should be here at present. If work had started—and it certainly looked as though it had, judging from the unusual activity—he was hardly likely to play an active role.

He might supervise from time to time, but she

doubted he'd want to get his hands dirty. She sighed. She should have gone to his house, after all. Despite her reluctance to set tongues wagging if she did.

She also knew she should have tried to contact him sooner.

It was nearly a month now since Sean had dragged her out to Jack's house. Nearly a month since she'd been embarrassed and humiliated. Nearly a month, and no word from Sean about paying her father back the money he'd borrowed.

And nearly a month since she'd assured herself she'd never see Jack Connolly again.

The way he'd looked at her! She shuddered at the memory. It was so obvious he'd thought she'd been as much to blame for what had happened as Sean.

Perhaps he'd even thought that that was why she'd practically thrown herself at him that morning at the cottage. It was certainly a possibility, despite her original reluctance to go with him.

So why had she come?

Grace thrust open the car door and got out.

It was a beautiful sunny morning, much different from the last time she was here. Even the church looked more appealing, the trees around it colourful now with blossom. And on the horizon, the sea looked bluer than she'd ever seen it.

She could smell the salt on the air, feel its scent coating her skin. And decided to walk along the cliff and see how the cottages were faring. She had nothing else to do until lunch.

As soon as she started along the cliff path she saw the Lexus.

It was parked a few yards from the cottages, with several other vehicles between it and a loaded skip.

Another pickup and two vans showed that work was already in progress, and Grace's determination faltered at the realisation that she wasn't going to be able to speak to Jack alone.

Her footsteps slowed. She might as well turn back, she thought. She wasn't supposed to be here, anyway. But her morning's viewing had finished early and she wasn't expected back in the office until half past one.

Then a man emerged from one of the cottages and saw her.

It wasn't Jack, but he came towards her, clearly wondering if she needed help. He was a good-looking man, in his late forties, she estimated, and she had the feeling that she'd seen him before.

'I shouldn't come any nearer,' he said, indicating the hard hat he was wearing. 'Health and Safety will have my guts for garters if I let you look around.'

Grace managed a faint smile, realising who he was at the same time that he recognised her.

'You're Tom Spencer's daughter, aren't you?' he exclaimed. 'I've seen you in the pub.'

Grace's smile got even thinner. 'Yes, that's right,' she mumbled now, wondering what the chances were of her meeting someone from Rothburn this far off the beaten track.

But, of course, it was like Jack to employ a builder he knew and approved of. Bob Grady's company had been partly responsible for the sympathetic renovation of Lindisfarne House.

'I knew it.' Grady looked pleased with his deduction. 'But what are you doing out here? You work for an estate agent these days, don't you? Don't tell me Jack has got the properties on the market already!'

'Oh, no. No!'

Grace couldn't let him think that, couldn't risk him going into the agency and mentioning her visit to Mr Hughes. It would be hard enough as it was, explaining her visit to her father. Because she had no doubt that Grady would mention it, the first chance he got.

'So, is it Jack you want to see?'

The man was persistent, but just then Grace had a brilliant idea.

'No,' she said, adopting a note of rueful innocence. 'But I was the one who showed Mr Connolly the cottages when he first became interested. As I was out this way, I thought I'd have a look and see how the development was progressing.'

'Ah.'

If Grady found her explanation just a tiny bit convenient, he didn't say so. Thankfully, he went on, before she could say something else to embarrass herself. 'As far as the development is concerned, it's hardly got off the ground.'

Grace's eyes widened. 'There's been a problem?'

'That's right.' Grady grimaced. 'We've found serious faults in the foundations and we may have to demolish most of the standing walls.'

Grace swallowed. 'I see.'

'Yeah.' Grady turned to survey the group of buildings behind him. 'Jack's brought another architect out to look at the place and he's consulting with him at present. He's got an idea that we might be able to pour concrete into the existing bedrock. That way we might not have to bulldoze the whole site.'

Grace shook her head. 'Is he very annoyed?' she murmured without thinking, and Grady gave her a curious look.

'Annoyed?' he echoed. 'Well, Jack's not pleased, I can tell you that. But if anyone can solve the problem, he can. He's won awards for developments he's designed in Ireland, you know.'

Grace hadn't known, but it didn't surprise her. She had the feeling that anything Jack did, he'd do well.

Incredibly well, she thought. Like making love to a woman. Something told her he'd be as expert at that as he was at everything else.

She shivered suddenly, in spite of the warmth of the day. She was remembering how it had felt to have his hands upon her, the raw sexuality of his mouth.

Oh, God, she thought, she had definitely not been wise to come here. Not when even the memory of his scent assaulted her senses, aroused an insistent need that hadn't been assuaged.

She was trying to remember what Grady had said so she could answer him, when the man spoke again.

'Here's Jack now,' he said. 'And that's the other architect with him. Let's hope they've got some good news. I don't want to have to lay my men off again.'

Grace's throat tightened at the sight of the two men walking towards them. She found it incredibly hard to breathe suddenly as she saw Jack recognise her. Particularly when there was no sign of welcome on his face.

He was wearing jeans again today, the same faded jeans she'd seen before, that hung low on his hips and emphasised his lean athletic frame.

A black cotton shirt, the sleeves turned back over sinewy forearms, hung half open and exposed the strong brown column of his throat.

Both men were wearing hard hats like Grady, but Jack hauled his off as they reached the parked vehicles. He opened the boot of the Lexus and tossed the hat inside.

His dark hair was untidy, evidence of the many times he'd raked his fingers through it. It had grown in the weeks since she'd seen him, and overlapped his collar by a couple of inches at the back.

'You've got a visitor, Jack,' Grady said, without waiting for Grace to introduce herself. 'She says she was the one who showed you the cottages in the first place.'

'Yeah. That's right.' Jack was too well-mannered to make any other response.

Grace squared her shoulders beneath her neatly buttoned shirt and met his gaze with a guarded stare.

'Mr Grady's been telling me you've found some problems,' she said politely. 'Perhaps you should take it up with Mrs Naughton. She might be prepared to buy the cottages back.'

'In a pig's eye,' said Jack succinctly and then turned to his builder. 'Ralph thinks we can use concrete to shore up the foundations. It's not as if we're planning on building a multistorey car park on the site.'

Grady's relief was palpable. 'Hell, that's great, Jack,' he said, grinning broadly. 'I'll get on to the yard right away. They should be able to fit us in at the beginning of next week.'

'You do that.'

Jack's eyes flickered over Grace's burning face before moving on to the man beside him.

'Thanks for your input, Ralph. It's much appreciated.'

'My pleasure.' The older man lifted a hand in a deprecatory gesture. 'You'd have done the same for me.' He glanced at his watch. 'I'd better get going. Goodbye, Bob. Goodbye, Ms Spencer.'

'Oh—goodbye.'

Grace was touched that he'd thought to include her in his farewells, particularly as Jack hadn't bothered to introduce them.

But then, she evidently wasn't Jack's favourite

person at the moment. She shifted uncomfortably. She shouldn't have come here. She should go, too.

'I'll come with you,' she called after Ralph's departing figure, unable to bring herself to use his name. It would have been too familiar.

However, Jack intervened. 'No, that's okay, Ralph,' he said as the other man turned. 'I want to have a word with Ms Spencer myself.' He nodded at Bob Grady as Ralph waved a hand before continuing on his way. 'Do you want to go and tell your men what's going on?'

'Oh—sure.'

Grady looked a little disappointed at being dismissed so arbitrarily. But, join the club, thought Grace, not exactly thrilled at Jack's arrogance herself.

Yet she couldn't deny the frisson of excitement she felt when Jack came towards her. Whatever way she might want to play this, she couldn't ignore his magnetism. Couldn't prevent her instinctive reaction to his dark masculine beauty.

CHAPTER TEN

'LET'S WALK,' JACK SAID, indicating the path that led past the row of cottages and out onto the cliff. 'I'd suggest we talk in my car, but I know we'd be observed.'

'And that matters to you?'

Grace spoke tartly, and Jack gave her a smouldering look.

'I'd assumed it would matter to you,' he said harshly, urging her to move forward. 'I'd rather not give Grady's men any more to gossip about in the Bay Horse tonight.'

'Oh, God!' Grace swallowed. 'Do you think they will?'

'It's a fair bet.' Jack was sardonic now.

Grace sighed. 'If I'd known you'd employed someone from Rothburn—'

'You wouldn't have come, I know.' Jack shrugged. 'It wasn't the most sensible idea you've ever had.'

Grace's throat tightened. 'I needed to speak to you.'

'I gathered that.'

He fell into step beside her as they passed the cottages and Grace was sure she could feel at least half a dozen pairs of eyes mapping their path. Jack seemed indifferent to her fears, however, adapting his long stride to the restrictions of her suit skirt. But even so, her high heels made it difficult to keep pace.

Beyond the cottages, the route became more uneven, unused in recent years except by walkers or children heading for the steps that led down to the cove.

The breeze was stronger here, but Grace was grateful for it. Despite opening the collar of her shirt, she could feel perspiration trickling down between her breasts.

'So,' he said, when they were safely out of earshot of their audience. 'Do you want to tell me what this is all about?'

Grace's tongue circled her dry lips and she couldn't resist glancing back over her shoulder. Jack wasn't touching her, but she was supremely aware of him, anyway. And she was sure that anyone watching them would be able to read her body language like an open book.

His warmth, his heat, enveloped her with an uncontrollable sensuality. The clean male scent of his body invading every susceptible pore of her skin.

They'd reached the rocky steps that zigzagged down the cliff to the cove, and Grace halted.

'Um—do you think we could go down to the beach?' she suggested, realising too late how provocative that must sound.

But at least they'd be out of sight of prying eyes,

she consoled herself. She didn't like the feeling of vulnerability she was experiencing at present.

Jack stared at her. Then his eyes dropped insolently down the length of her body. Their darkness deepened as they moved over her neat white shirt and narrow black skirt. And her legs in transparent black tights wobbled uncertainly.

'Can you see yourself going down those steps in those heels?' he asked incredulously.

And she breathed a little more easily when his gaze returned to her face.

'I can take my shoes off,' she said at once, bending to do so with more bravado than sense. 'There. You see!' she added. 'No problem.'

Despite her assertion, Jack suspected he should refuse her request and insist they remain on the cliff top. At least up here he could kid himself he retained a modicum of good sense.

He'd been down to the cove only once before, but he knew it would be deserted at this time of day. It was unlikely that anyone would brave the water. Despite its beauty, the sea was cold.

He'd be crazy to agree.

Nevertheless, he found himself saying, 'Okay. But I'll go ahead. Just in case it's not as easy as you think.'

Grace nodded, feeling a little breathless before she'd even started. Which was ridiculous, really. The hard part would be climbing back up again.

Jack, in rubber-soled trainers, had no problem

with the steps. They were uneven, but fairly easy to negotiate, so long as he didn't look back.

On the rare occasions when he did—just to check that she was all right, he assured himself—the view was tantalising. Beneath her skirt, long legs stretched provocatively up to her crotch.

Grace had her own troubles to contend with.

The urge to use Jack's shoulder as a crutch being the most insistent. She knew that beneath his shirt, his skin would feel warm and reassuring. And if she slipped…

But she restrained those thoughts, concentrating instead on keeping her feet. Unfortunately, in her bid to appear unconcerned, she hadn't given any thought to fallen stones or broken edges. By the time she stepped down onto the sand, her tights had been shredded in a dozen different places.

Jack was waiting for her and the wry amusement in his gaze was the last straw.

'Just turn away,' she snapped, and, when he did, she ripped off the offending articles, stuffing them into the toes of one of her shoes before saying, 'All right. You can look now.'

It wasn't the most sensible thing she might have said, but she doubted anything would have stopped Jack from staring at her. And without her tights, she definitely felt more exposed. Unlike his skin, her legs looked pale and uninteresting, a stark contrast to the darkness of her skirt.

'Are you okay?' he asked, his eyes narrowing

slightly, and she wondered what he was really thinking when he looked at her.

That for someone who was supposed to be going out with another man, she was absurdly reckless with her reputation? Whatever puerile excuse had brought her out here?

'I'm good,' she said now, putting her shoes down at the foot of the steps and smoothing nervous fingers over her skirt.

Grace pushed her toes into the sand to avoid looking at him. She'd decided it would be easier to say what she had to say if they weren't standing face-to-face.

Jack surveyed the cove that was little more than half a mile from end to end. 'Let's go this way. I believe there are some caves near the rocks.'

'Caves!'

The word escaped on a squeak that Grace managed to disguise by clearing her throat.

But, heavens, she didn't want to go caving with him. Even if the idea did have its temptations.

She frowned then. She wasn't here to repeat past mistakes, she reminded herself severely. She just wanted Jack to understand that Sean's request for finance had nothing to do with her.

'Yes, caves.' Apparently Jack hadn't noticed her exclamation. 'According to one of the locals, they used to connect with a tunnel from some castle near here.'

'Really?'

Grace tried to sound interested, but her awareness of him had jumped to a new level since they'd reached the beach. Without her heels, he was so much bigger than she was, for one thing. And for another, his apparent ability to ignore what had happened between them previously caught her on the raw.

'The guy says the tunnel's been blocked off now because of the dangers of a roof fall,' Jack continued on, regardless. 'Or that's his story. Who knows? Maybe smuggling still goes on along this coast.'

Grace cleared her throat again. 'I—I doubt it's a big concern in these parts,' she murmured, trying to match his detachment. 'The tides are too unstable. And there are currents under the water.'

She forced a smile. 'Besides, some of the locals love to tell a good tale.'

Jack glanced sideways at her. Then his brows drew together. 'What's the matter, Grace? Wishing you'd stayed where we were?'

'No!'

'Sure?' Jack sounded sceptical. 'You're not worried about what might happen now we're alone together?'

Grace's jaw dropped. 'No!'

'That's good.' Jack nodded. 'Because I can tell you you've got nothing to fear from me.'

Never mind what Grace was thinking, he was regretting giving in to her suggestion to come down here. It was so remote, so isolated. And whatever he'd told her, at least one part of his body wasn't listening to his brain.

He sensed rather than heard Grace coming after him.

'Did I say I didn't trust you?' she demanded, and now he could hear that she was out of breath.

What she wasn't aware of was that with every gulp of air she took, the lapels on her shirt gaped invitingly. But she was too busy trying to convince him that she had a handle on the situation to notice it.

'Okay, no,' he said now, dragging his eyes away from that tempting cleft between her breasts. 'So long as we understand one another.'

Yeah, right.

Grace's cheeks were pink, as much with the way she was feeling as with exertion. 'I—I needed to talk to you, that's all.'

'You keep saying that.' Jack regarded her with an expectant expression. 'So why don't you go ahead and talk? I'm listening.'

Grace pursed her lips. 'It's not that easy.'

'Isn't it?' Jack pulled a wry face. 'I haven't noticed you having a problem before.'

Grace trudged on for a while in silence.

Then she halted and said, 'Do you blame me because the cottages are going to be far more expensive to restore?'

It was such a non sequitur that Jack blinked.

'Uh—no,' he said, halting in his tracks to look at her. Then, his brows drawing together, 'Are you saying that Hughes knew there were structural problems when he took them on?'

'No.' Grace was anxious now. 'Mrs Naughton might have. But she's an old woman. She probably hasn't been inside any of the buildings for years.'

'Okay.' Jack stared at her.

Grace pressed her lips together. Why didn't she just admit that the real reason she'd come to see him was to exonerate herself from any resentment he might be feeling towards Sean?

Because that would be far too disloyal, even for her.

Grace was silent for so long that Jack expelled a weary breath. It was obvious she had something else on her mind, but for some reason she was finding it difficult to voice.

He suspected Sean was involved. He couldn't think of any other reason why she might be so hesitant. Which made him somewhat less than gracious when he said, 'What's the matter, Grace? Wasn't the hundred thousand I loaned Sean enough?'

Grace's mouth dried. 'You—you loaned Sean one hundred thousand pounds?'

Jack didn't answer. He was already regretting making such an admission to her.

Instead, he turned and stared out at the ocean. It was amazingly blue, and so calm the horizon shimmered in a haze of heat.

Much different from the first time he'd come here. He sighed. He really didn't want to be having this conversation. Not with someone who evidently had such a vested interest in its outcome.

Couldn't Sean fight his own battles, if that was what this was all about? Instead of sending a woman to do a man's work?

Did he think—did he suspect—that she might have more success than he would?

And if so, what did that say for Sean's relationship with Grace? Jack hadn't forgotten that strange conversation about her that Sean had initiated at his house.

'Look,' he said at last, turning to face her again. 'It's no big deal, right? I went into it with my eyes open. But you can tell your boyfriend, that's it! I'm not investing any more in his company, not until he proves to me he knows what the hell he's doing.'

Grace's head moved jerkily from side to side. She looked stunned, he thought. Stunned and disbelieving. Hell, did she think he was lying to her?

Her next words reassured him. On that score, at least.

'I—I don't know what to say,' she mumbled.

And he had to steel himself against the distress that was filling her green eyes with tears.

'I didn't know how…how much he'd asked you to lend him,' she whispered, fumbling in her bag for a tissue and blowing her nose. 'Honestly, I had no idea.'

Jack wanted to believe her. But she was Sean's

girlfriend. Obviously she owed him more loyalty than she owed Jack.

Besides, surely to God she'd realised what he and Sean had been talking about when she'd been left to kick her heels in his living room at Lindisfarne House?

'Okay,' he said finally.

But she must have heard the scepticism in his voice because her eyes were suddenly filled with pain.

'You don't believe me,' she exclaimed, and he was almost sure no one could look so innocent and be lying through their teeth.

'Dammit, Grace,' he said, reaching for her arms, torn by her vulnerability.

But she backed away from him. She winced when her foot encountered another of the sharp stones she'd had to contend with on her way down the steps, but she didn't falter.

'Don't—' she said unsteadily. 'Don't you dare feel sorry for me.'

Jack groaned. 'I don't,' he said harshly, coming after her. So that when she felt the rough wall of the cliff at her back, she had no way of escape.

'Grace,' he said again, supporting himself with a hand at either side of her head, trapping her. He looked down into her eyes, his dark and sensual between thick black lashes. 'Why the hell couldn't you have left well enough alone?'

'Not come here, you mean?' she asked huskily, and his acknowledgement was impatient.

'That's the least of it,' he said, and, lowering his head, he took her mouth.

She tasted just as lush and wet and sensuous as he remembered. Her lips were parted and he didn't hesitate before pushing his tongue inside.

She opened wider to admit him, and he bent his arms at the elbows so that he could brush her body with his. The hard nubs of her breasts were taut against his chest and the temptation was to crush her against the rock face behind her and let her feel what she was doing to him.

But he knew if he did that, he couldn't answer for the consequences, and he still had some self-respect.

Yet, despite the love he'd had for Lisa, he knew no other woman had ever had such an effect on him. He felt both a need to protect her and an urgent desire to make love with her, his aching arousal threatening to drag him to his knees.

'This is crazy,' he said thickly, releasing her mouth to press his face into the hollow of her neck. She was trembling, and that only added to the sense of responsibility he was feeling.

'I—I know,' she breathed, and when he lifted his head, her eyes were wide with a mixture of uncertainty and anticipation.

'Then we should go,' said Jack, but he didn't move. Couldn't move, he thought incredulously, and when she lifted a hand to cup his face, he shuddered un-controllably.

His jawline was rough with at least a couple of days' growth of beard, but Grace loved the feel of his stubble against her fingers. Loved, too, the way he turned his head and bestowed a lingering kiss on her palm.

Then, with a groan, he gripped her chin and turned her face up to his. This time, his mouth was hot and hungry, and she had no defence against such deliberate sexuality.

She responded willingly, eagerly, uncaring where they were or who might see them. She lifted her arms and wound them round his neck, sliding her fingers into his hair and fisting the damp curls at the nape of his neck.

She arched away from the rock face, pressing her-self against him, and felt the unmistakeable thrust of his erection. And wished his body could imitate the tantalising invasion of his tongue.

Jack felt the wilful response of her body with a feeling of desperation. This wasn't supposed to hap-pen, he told himself, even as his fingers traced the hollow beneath her ear, probed inside the neckline of her shirt.

She was wearing a bra, but it was only a delicate shred of lace that gave easily beneath the determined pressure of his hand. And then her breasts were spill-ing out of her shirt, the buttons parting with little effort on his part.

'God,' he muttered, bending lower to take one swollen nipple into his mouth. 'You are so...beautiful!'

Grace caught her breath as his tongue curled around the sensitive peak and sucked on it. She felt both weak and powerful, her legs trembling with the effort of remaining upright beneath his sensual assault.

Jack tried to hang on to some semblance of sanity, but it was a losing battle. Her feel, her touch, her taste, made any kind of resistance futile, and when he found her mouth again, he knew there could be no turning back.

His hands gripped her hips, urging her back against the cliff as he rocked his throbbing arousal against her yielding body. And felt her part her legs to bring him even closer.

Now his hands found the hem of that prim little skirt, forcing it upwards. His hands slid against cool feminine thighs, against skin as smooth and inviting as silk.

'I want you,' he bit out unsteadily, and she looked up at him with unguarded eyes.

'I want you, too,' she breathed, the words barely audible, and with a muffled oath he pushed her lacy briefs down her legs.

'Here?' he demanded, and she nodded.

'Yes, here,' she said unsteadily, and Jack closed his eyes for a moment, praying for deliverance.

But it never came.

Instead, he felt her fingers unfastening his belt buckle, unzipping his jeans and then taking him in her hot little hands.

Jack's groan was anguished, but he was already lifting her against him. He encouraged her to wind her legs about his hips, pulling himself out of her hands to push into hot, wet nirvana.

Grace sucked in a breath as his thick shaft penetrated her, invaded her, stretching her and filling her in a way she'd never experienced before.

Feeling his length inside her, pulsing deep against her womb, aroused sensations that both scared and delighted her. Her mind went dizzy with visions of spinning out across an endless ocean, of riding on angels' wings, heading irresistibly towards the sun.

Jack drove into her again, withdrawing just enough to leave her weak and begging for more. Her nails dug into his shoulders, and she wanted to tear the shirt from him. But she had to be content with pushing her fingers inside his collar, feeling smooth brown skin beneath her hands.

Again and again, he drove into her until her body felt as if it were on fire. As if the need he had created could only be assuaged if they both went up in flames.

And then it happened.

Just when she thought she couldn't take any more, her body exploded around him. She floated out on waves of ecstasy, the force of her orgasm driving Jack completely over the edge.

He would have withdrawn from her then and spilled himself on the sand. But Grace wouldn't let him.

With a strength she'd hardly known she possessed, she wound herself even tighter about him. She wanted to prolong this moment, wanted to share his release as he had shared hers.

And then, it was far too late for Jack to do anything but slump heavily against her. He shuddered his seed into her waiting body and prayed to Jude, the patron saint of lost causes, that God might forgive this mortal fool…

CHAPTER ELEVEN

'WHERE ON EARTH have you been?'

It was after midnight when Jack got home. And, having spent the past six hours trying to numb his senses with alcohol, he was in no mood for Lisa's accusations.

'Get lost,' he growled, but he could hear the slur in his voice and he knew Lisa would hear it, too.

'Ew, you're drunk!' she exclaimed disgustedly. 'I don't know what's the matter with you, Jack. You never used to care so little about your health.'

Jack wasn't inclined to debate the issue. Slamming the heavy door behind him, he fumbled to secure the deadbolt. It took a few attempts, but at last the key turned in the lock and he sank back against the door, preparing himself to climb the stairs.

Then, without bothering to put on any lights, he started across the hall.

To his relief, Lisa seemed to have given up on him and he wasn't sorry. He was bone-tired. Exhausted, actually. He couldn't wait to strip off his clothes and crawl into bed.

Not that he truly expected to sleep. His mind was still buzzing with the events of the afternoon at Culworth, his senses still humming with what he told himself was the best sex he'd ever had.

But that was exactly why he'd spent so long in the pub. Not her father's pub, of course, but another, smaller, hostelry in the next village. He'd hoped he might erase those events from his mind, temporarily at least.

It hadn't happened.

The memory of Grace's mouth, Grace's body, Grace's sensual sweetness, filled his thoughts to the exclusion of anything else.

But it was wrong; so wrong. Even now, after so many hours of soul-searching, he couldn't begin to comprehend what he'd been thinking of.

Okay, she hadn't exactly resisted him, but that was no excuse for the way he'd behaved. For pity's sake, he'd hit her with Sean's demand and then taken advantage of her stunned reaction to it.

She'd needed comfort, not seduction. Tender understanding, not the raw passion of someone who apparently cared little for her sensitivities and even less for Sean's.

Sean!

He felt sick at the thought of what he'd done to Sean. All right, there was no doubt that he and Sean had drifted apart in recent years, and their goals were not the same any longer.

But he was still Grace's boyfriend; still the man he assumed she would marry.

And yet, today at least, Grace hadn't behaved as if she'd felt guilty for what had happened. On the contrary, she'd responded to his lovemaking with an eagerness and a sensuality that aroused him still. He doubted he'd ever be able to look down on that stretch of sand again without recalling what had happened there in intimate detail.

It was the shriek of gulls that had brought him to his senses. Drunk with passion, reeling from emotions he'd never expected or wanted to feel, it had been an actual effort to drag himself away from her. He hadn't wanted to do it, and, judging from the way she'd clung to him, she hadn't wanted it, either.

He remembered she'd given a little moan of protest as he'd attempted to restore her clothes to some sort of order. And he hadn't been able to resist kissing her again, tasting once more the lush sweetness he'd found with his tongue.

God, what had she been thinking? What had he been thinking? He must have been mad.

Mad with lust, certainly, and blinded by his own selfish desires.

Whatever, they'd eventually walked back along the beach to where she'd left her shoes. He hadn't expected she would have anything to say to him, but in the aftermath of passion, she'd found her voice.

'I—I want you to know, I didn't intend for this to happen,' she'd told him quietly. 'And I don't blame you. I don't blame you at all.'

She'd sighed then. 'I'd just wanted you to know that it wasn't my idea to approach you for...for money. For the past month, I've been trying to

summon up the courage to apologise for Sean's...
behaviour.'

Sean!

Yeah, right.

At that moment, Jack had felt like the lowest form
of pond life. If he'd taken her earlier admission at
face value—if he'd believed her, in other words—
this wouldn't have happened.

It had occurred to him—belatedly—that maybe
that was why she'd allowed him to—

But no. Grace was not venal; he'd known it would
never have occurred to her to use her body as a
means to an end.

He couldn't remember what he'd said to her then.
He did remember climbing the steps, giving her his
hand when she'd let out a cry of pain because a peb-
ble had dug into her foot.

And ultimately asking those fatal questions:

Did she love Sean?

And if not, why did she stay with him?

She hadn't answered him. With eyes that were
suspiciously bright, she'd simply balled up her tights
and pushed them into her bag before slipping her
feet into her shoes.

It was that action, as much as anything, that had
made him realise that really nothing had changed.
It was as if by putting on her shoes she had drawn a
line under the reckless events of the day.

And he'd still had no idea how she was really feeling, deep inside.

He remembered escorting her to her car. After she'd driven away, he supposed he'd been in a state of shock. Disgusted with himself, definitely. But what was worse had been the realisation that the feelings she'd aroused were not going away.

The urge had been to go and get drunk, to bury his sorrows in the bottom of a bottle of Scotch. But instead he'd decided he needed physical exertion, and he'd spent the next couple of hours using a sledgehammer to break up the flags in the kitchen of one of the cottages they were working on.

He guessed the men were curious about his uncharacteristic behaviour. He only hoped Bob Grady wouldn't go blabbing about it in the Bay Horse. He didn't care for himself but Grace's name was bound to be mentioned.

By late afternoon, he'd been unable to control himself any longer. He'd had to try to speak to Grace again. He'd needed closure. He'd told himself he was doing it to salve his conscience, but the truth was he'd been desperate to hear her voice.

Had he hoped for absolution? If so, he'd been disappointed. When he'd rung the agency, Elizabeth Fleming had told him that Grace had phoned to say she wasn't well and was taking the rest of the day off.

Elizabeth had obviously been curious to know why he wanted to speak to Grace. But although he'd known Grace must have a mobile phone, there was no way Mrs Fleming would have given that number to him.

Not that he'd asked her to.

And as for ringing the Bay Horse…

That was how he'd ended up at a strange pub. But the relief he'd been seeking wasn't there. All he'd found was a curdling stomach and a pounding head. And more self-disgust than he could cope with.

The sudden switching on of a light bewildered him.

He was halfway up the stairs and he groped weakly for the banister, clinging to the wood for dear life.

'Dammit, Lisa,' he swore, even though she'd never accomplished such a thing before. 'Give me a break!'

'Oh, Jack!'

The sympathetic voice was both familiar and unfamiliar. And when he looked up it was to find Debra Carrick standing at the top of the stairs, her hand still on the switch.

'Oh, Jack,' she said again, wrapping the folds of her cotton dressing gown more closely about her plump little body. 'I thought you came here to get over Lisa. But it sounds to me as if it isn't working.'

Jack groaned.

This was all he needed. Lisa's little sister come to help him lick his wounds.

Wounds he no longer had, he realised belatedly. Even without what had happened between him and Grace, the pain he'd felt when Lisa died had—like his late wife—passed away.

'I'm good, Debs,' he assured his sister-in-law firmly, straightening away from the banister.

Or he would be, once he'd closed his bedroom door.

'But you were calling for Lisa,' she protested. 'I heard you.' Her eyes grew misty. 'I told your mother you'd welcome some company despite what you said.'

Jack blew out a breath.

Was there any point in denying he'd used Lisa's name?

'You're imagining things,' he said. And then, in an attempt to divert her, 'Anyway, what are you doing here?' His brows drew together in sudden confusion. 'How the hell did you get in?'

'Oh—some woman was still here when I arrived,' declared Debra easily. 'I think she said her name was Honeyman. Is that right?'

'Mrs Honeyman, yes.' Jack frowned. 'But she usually leaves at midday.'

'She did.' Debra started down the stairs towards him and Jack was obliged to back up himself to avoid her. 'I've been here since about half past eleven. I flew into Newcastle this morning and got a taxi from the airport to the house.'

Jack, who had been backing down the stairs, reached the bottom without warning. The sudden impact caused him to stagger a little and Debra hurried down the last few stairs to wrap her arms about his waist.

'It's okay,' she said, as if he were some child in danger of falling. And then the alcohol on his breath caused her to step back in dismay.

'You've been drinking,' she exclaimed. 'Oh, Jack, I'm so glad I didn't take your mother's advice and stay away.'

You should have done!

The words hovered on Jack's tongue, but he didn't utter them. Extricating himself from lingering fingers, he turned rather desperately towards the kitchen.

His mother should have phoned, he thought. She should have warned him Debra was coming. Instead of leaving him to deal with a female who evidently thought he was in danger of falling apart.

'D'you want coffee?' he asked.

'At this time of night?' Debra had followed him into the kitchen, and Jack quickly put the island between them. 'Oughtn't you to have something to eat?'

'I'm not hungry.'

In actual fact, Jack hadn't had anything to eat since breakfast. And right now, the thought of food nauseated him. But however unwelcome her arrival, Debra was a guest, and he was obliged to make the requisite response.

'Have you eaten?'

'Oh, yes.' Debra nodded. 'Mrs Honeyman made me some soup at lunchtime. And she said to tell you, she's left a steak pie in the fridge.' She shrugged. 'I hope you don't mind, I made myself an omelette at dinner time. I suppose I could have cooked the pie, but I didn't know what time you'd be back.'

Jack nodded. Knowing Mrs Honeyman as he did, he doubted she'd have been best pleased to find they had an unexpected visitor.

Jack switched the coffee on and then turned to prop his hips rather wearily against the dishwasher.

'So,' he said, when she was unexpectedly silent. 'Come on, Debs. Why are you here?'

Debra's lips, a fuller version of her sister's, pursed defensively. 'I should have thought that was obvious,' she said, her expression showing she'd been hurt by the question. 'We're all worried about you.'

Jack sighed. 'Who's we?'

'Your father, your mother.' She hesitated before adding, 'Francis.'

Jack sighed. 'You're wrong, Debs.' He shook his head. 'Ma and Pa aren't worried about me. They know I'm happy here, doing what I want, making a life for myself somewhere new and different. And as for Francis…' his brother '…he's a priest. He doesn't have time to worry about me.'

'Maeve, then,' retorted Debra tartly. 'Did you know she's pregnant? Again?'

Jack hid a grin.

'I think you've answered your own question there, Debs. My sister has a husband and two little girls to care about. Not to mention a new baby on the way. If her brother is too…bullheaded…or too selfish to keep in touch with her, she probably thinks he doesn't deserve her.'

'You know she doesn't think like that.'

'I know.'

Jack knew that was true. Despite the distance between them, they'd always been a close family. Always there for each other when they were needed.

But Debra wasn't family. Not really. And he suspected Debra's reasons for coming here weren't entirely disinterested.

'Anyway,' he said, turning to pour himself a mug of coffee, 'shouldn't you be in school?'

Debra snorted. 'I'm at college, Jack.' She was indignant. 'And it's summer break, as if you didn't know.'

Jack stifled a groan.

'So—what?' he said, turning back, deciding to take his coffee black to try to clear his head. 'Is this the start of a European tour?'

'No!' Debra stared at him impatiently. 'I've just told you, I've come to look after you, Jack. I'm sure you're not looking after yourself properly.'

Jack blew on his coffee before taking an unwary gulp. It was much too hot and it burned his mouth, but at least the pain achieved what a gallon of alcohol couldn't.

'You can't stay here, Debs,' he said, trying to sound mature and reasonable.

But for pity's sake, he didn't want to be accused

of taking advantage of a young girl. He had enough
on his conscience as it was.

Debra looked shocked now. 'Why can't I stay
here?' she exclaimed indignantly. 'You need someone, Jack. Someone who knows you and cares about
you.'

'No.' Jack was adamant. 'No, I don't.' He paused
and then added as gently as he could, 'It would be
different if we were related. But we're not. And can
you imagine what people would say if they found
out I was living with an attractive young female like
yourself?'

Debra's expression softened. 'Do you think I'm
attractive, Jack?'

Jack blew out a weary breath.

'Of course I think you're attractive,' he said. But
when she would have moved towards him, he held
up a hand to stop her. 'But you're Lisa's little sister, Debs. I'm sorry. You'll never mean more to me
than that.'

Debra looked sulky now. 'How do you know?'

'I just do.'

'And since when have you cared what people
think?' she persisted, trying another approach. 'Lisa
said you never listened to gossip.'

'I don't—'

'Then—'

'But other people do,' finished Jack flatly. 'Come
on, Debs. It's not the end of the world. I can't be-

lieve you came all this way just to tell me you cared about me.'

'Why not?'

'Because—well, because you're too young, for one thing. And what about that boy you were seeing in Kilpheny? Wasn't his name Brendan or something?'

'Brendan Foyle,' agreed Debra, plucking at the ends of her belt. 'But like you said, he's just a boy. I'm not interested in *boys*!'

Jack felt horribly old suddenly.

He was tired and the last thing he needed was to have to deal with a lovesick adolescent. Debra was—what? Nineteen? Twenty? Her parents should have had more sense than to let her come here.

'I think I ought to give your mother a call in the morning and tell her you're on your way home,' he said at last.

But Debra looked horrified at this suggestion.

'Mummy doesn't know I'm here,' she exclaimed. 'Nor does Daddy. I told them I was going to stay with your parents. I was going to tell them where I really was in a few days.'

'Well, now you won't have to,' said Jack reasonably. 'If you get a flight back to Dublin in the morning, they need never know you've been here. And I'm sure Ma and Pa will be only too happy to see you.' He crossed his fingers as he said this. 'And Maeve, too. I dare say she'd be glad of a babysitter.'

Debra looked mutinous. 'You don't care about me

at all, do you? I'm just a nuisance, turning up like this. Well, I was going to tell you something that might make you feel a bit better, but now I don't think I will.'

Jack shook his head. 'I doubt if anything you told me could make me feel better,' he said bitterly.

After the day he'd had, even being told he'd won the lottery wouldn't cut it.

'It was about Lisa.'

Debra clearly had no intention of keeping the information to herself.

But did Jack really want to hear it?

'So—what about Lisa?' he asked at last, realising Debra wasn't about to go to bed without delivering her message. 'If it's something to do with the accident, I'd really rather not hear another version of how it was all her fault—'

'She wasn't alone,' said Debra impulsively, and Jack could only stare at her with uncomprehending eyes.

'What do you mean, she wasn't alone? Of course she was alone. My God, didn't I have to listen to all that testimony at the inquest? The details of how they'd found only one person's remains in the ashes of the car? Don't you think they'd have told me if there'd been more than one fatality? For God's sake, Debra, your sister's dead. Leave it be.'

'She wasn't alone,' persisted Debra doggedly. 'You can rail at me all you want, but I'm not lying.' She licked her lips. 'The man—the man she was with was thrown clear. Just like that sandal they found that belonged to Lisa.' She took a deep breath. 'She was having an affair, Jack. And I thought you deserved to know the truth.'

CHAPTER TWELVE

A WEEK LATER, Grace got a phone call from Sean.

It was five weeks since she'd seen him; five weeks since he'd returned to London, ostensibly to set up the website Jack Connolly had invested in.

Grace had spent part of the time looking for an apartment in Rothburn. She could have got one in Alnwick easily enough, but she wanted to be near her parents if they needed her.

That part of her reason for moving north hadn't changed. Even if so much else in her life had.

Unfortunately, she hadn't been successful. Apartments in Rothburn were hard to find. And she'd had to contend with both her mother and her father assuring her that she could stay at the pub for the foreseeable future. They'd even talked about adding a small extension if the deal her father had with Sean was a success.

For her part, Grace had been in no hurry to hear from him again, unless it was to say he had managed to recover her parents' investment. Goodness knew the money Jack had given him would have gone a long way to repaying the mortgage on the pub. But she could have hardly said that to him without sounding as if she wanted a share.

And she really didn't want to be in Jack's debt.

She hadn't heard from Jack in the past week, either. But that hadn't surprised her. Despite the thrill the memory of that scene on the beach still caused, common sense told her that entertaining any real feelings for a man who was still mourning the death of his wife was plain stupid.

Besides, she was kidding herself if she thought he cared about her. If he'd had any respect for her feelings, he'd never have seduced her when he believed she was still involved with Sean.

But had she given him a choice?

How tempted she'd been to tell Jack the truth about her and Sean's relationship. To admit that the man was selfish, egotistical, that he'd lied about everything she'd ever believed about him.

She would have liked to tell Jack about the so-called business trips abroad that Sean had said would advance his knowledge of computer gaming. That it was only by chance that she'd discovered his latest trip to Las Vegas had not been made alone.

He'd been stringing her a line, and she'd been too stupid—or too naïve—to realise it. It wasn't until she'd actually found him in bed with one of her girlfriends that she'd realised he'd been using her, just as he'd used everyone else.

That was when she'd told him she was going back to Rothburn. She couldn't go on living with a man who had no respect for her at all. He'd objected, of course, and when his pleas for her forgiveness had come to nothing, he'd threatened to tell her parents that he was broke.

That news had sickened her. Despite her contempt for the way he'd behaved, she'd still believed he was trying to get his business off the ground. He'd insisted that he was still making progress, but learning that he'd spent her parents' money as well as hers was devastating.

Consequently, she couldn't explain why she didn't break up with Sean without admitting how her father had been cheated. And with her mother only now recovering from what might have been a terminal illness, how could she risk Tom Spencer finding out?

Just recently, her father had actually asked when she thought Sean might start making some money from his investment, and Grace had had to bite her tongue and admit she didn't know.

No, although she'd cried herself to sleep some nights, she'd decided it was safer to stick to her original plan and avoid all complications. Telling Jack her troubles would sound too much like hitting on him herself.

It was early evening when the phone rang.

She'd taken to turning off her mobile phone when she got home in the evenings, so it was the phone just outside the bar that her father answered.

'It's Sean,' he said, and, although her heart sank, she could tell he was pleased. 'He says he can't get you on your mobile, and I explained you'd probably left it upstairs and couldn't hear it.' He gestured towards the hall behind him. 'Go on. Ask him when we're going to see him.'

Not soon, thought Grace bitterly. She could imagine he'd spent the past five weeks spending Jack's money. Was he broke again? Was that why he was calling her? If only she could shut him out of her life.

'What does he want?' she asked, and her father looked scandalised.

'I didn't ask him,' he said shortly. 'It's you he wants to speak to, not me.'

'Well, I don't want to speak to him,' she muttered, but her father heard her.

'You don't mean that,' he said. 'Besides, he may have some good news about the website.'

As always, her father believed everything Sean said.

'Anyway...' Tom Spencer scowled '... I hope your attitude towards Sean isn't because of that man, Connolly.' He snorted. 'He's not interested in you, Grace. Apart from the fact that he's just lost his wife, the kind of money he's got to play around with, he won't be staying around here long. We're far too countrified for him.'

'Gee, thanks!'

Grace was hurt that her father could dismiss her so easily. Hurt, too, that he didn't think she had it in her to attract a man like Jack.

She wondered what he'd say if she told him she'd already had sex with Jack. It would certainly prove she wasn't the small-town innocent he was trying to imply.

Unfortunately, it might also prove that she'd learned nothing from her relationship with Sean, she reflected dourly. But she wished he and her mother would stop trying to push her into Sean's arms.

'You know what I mean,' her father said now, evidently regretting his candour. 'I just don't want you to get hurt.'

'You don't think Sean might have hurt me, do you? What if I told you Sean already had hurt me? How would you feel about that?'

'I'd say it was just a misunderstanding,' averred Mr Spencer, turning away with some relief when a customer snagged his attention. 'Anyway,' he added, taking a glass from the shelf above his head, 'go and have a word with him. I've told him you're here, so I can't go and lie to him, can I?'

'You could,' muttered Grace as she reluctantly passed through the door into the hall of the pub. 'But you won't,' she added, grudgingly picking up the phone.

'Say what?' Sean had evidently heard her grumbling to herself but hadn't been able to distinguish the words. 'Is that you, baby?'

Grace wasn't in the mood to be amenable. 'What do you want, Sean? I thought we'd said all there was to say the last time you were here.'

'Don't be like that, Grace.' Sean sounded hurt, but

she wasn't falling for that. 'Come on, sweetheart. Haven't you missed me just the tiniest little bit?'

'Uh—no.' Grace was candid. 'Why don't you tell me what you want? You didn't ring to ask about my health.'

'Well, no.' Sean went silent for a moment, and then he said carefully, 'I've got Jack's financial advisor on my back. He wants to know why I haven't sent him a copy of the contract yet.'

Grace sighed. 'You must have expected that. Jack Connolly's not going to be as easy to deceive as Dad.'

'Grace, Grace. You know I'm doing this as much for you as me and—'

'No!'

'Well, your parents, then. I need your help, baby.' He paused. 'Don't let me down.'

Was there a threat in those words? Grace felt an uneasy shiver slide down her spine. 'I can't help you, Sean. I don't have any money. And if you think I'm going to ask Dad to take out a second mortgage…'

'No, no. I know your parents don't have any money.'

Sean was scornful. 'I used to think pubs were gold mines, but obviously I was wrong.' He took a breath. 'I want you to go and see Jack. Tell him I'm doing my best to get things moving. I need you to explain to him that these things take time.'

'I can't do that.'

Grace was adamant. Although the idea of having a

legitimate reason to see Jack again caused her heart to thump almost audibly against her ribs.

'Yes, you can.' Sean had always been persistent. 'He likes you, babe. I know he does. You're just the person to keep him sweet.'

'To keep him sweet?'

Grace was horrified. What did Sean expect her to do?

'The guy thinks you're hot,' he went on, taking her reaction at its face value. 'You're a clever girl, Grace. And it's not as if I'm asking you to sleep with him or anything.'

Too bad, thought Grace bitterly. Been there, done that, bought the tee shirt.

'I just want you to be nice to him,' he continued wheedlingly. Then, when she didn't say anything, his attitude changed. 'Or would you rather have him haul me to court?'

'To court?' Grace was taken aback.

Sean was losing his cool rapidly. 'I'm not saying he would do it but his financial advisor wants things doing all legal and official-like.' He snorted. 'I don't do business that way. Besides, I thought Jack was a friend.'

Grace blew out a breath. She might want nothing more to do with Sean, but she didn't want him to be hauled into court. How could she hide that from her parents? Even if Sean let her try.

After a moment, she said, 'Why can't you just do

as he asks and draw up a contract? You have a friend who's a solicitor, don't you?'

'And how much do you think that would cost?' demanded Sean irritably. 'Okay, if you refuse to help me, I'll have to think of something else. But I doubt your parents will be too pleased when they find out you had a chance to save the damn website and you refused to do it.'

'Sean—'

But he'd already rung off, and Grace replaced the receiver with a slightly trembling hand,

She stood for a moment, trying to calm herself. He wouldn't tell her parents. But he was just spiteful enough to try if he didn't get his own way.

She groaned. If she hadn't invited him up to Rothburn, her father would never have got involved. And Sean would never have known where Jack was living. It was all her fault; both the fact of her father's participation and Sean contacting Jack again.

Though not her fault he'd asked Jack for money, she told herself. Not her fault that he hadn't kept his part of the bargain he'd made with Jack.

And what kind of man asked a girl he was supposed to love to be nice to someone just for a business deal? She could answer her own question. The kind of man who'd slept with another woman in their bed.

He didn't know she'd seen Jack again. He didn't know how intimate their relationship had become.

Which was exactly the reason why she felt guilty.

She wasn't the innocent pushover he believed her to be.

Without telling her father where she was going, she ran upstairs to her bedroom. Slamming the door, she seated herself at the vanity and stared at her reflection.

Tear-wet eyes stared back at her, dark lashes shading their fractured depths. But her tears weren't for Sean, she thought, scrubbing her cheeks impatiently. The bewilderment she felt was all about herself.

Abruptly, turning her back on the mirror, she surveyed the room with wild eyes. Where was her mobile phone? There, on the cabinet beside the bed.

Snatching it up, she speed-dialled Sean's number before she could change her mind again. She'd go and see Jack, she decided. However painful it was going to be, she felt she couldn't do anything else.

When a woman answered her call, she was taken aback.

'Yes,' the woman said. 'Sean Nesbitt's phone. Who is this?'

'As if you don't know,' said Grace harshly.

It was Natalie West, she realised. The girl who'd professed to be her friend and then slept with Sean. It seemed that despite his pleas of loyalty, Sean was still involved with the other woman.

There was a moment's muttered conversation and then Sean came on the line, apologising fervently.

'Sorry about that,' he said. 'I've got a couple of friends round and one of them picked up the phone.'

'It was Natalie,' said Grace bluntly. 'I recognised her voice and I'm pretty sure she recognised mine. You know, I wish I'd never made this call. You don't change. You never will.'

'Grace!' He sounded desperate now. 'You can't blame me for dating someone else when you won't even let me near you.'

Grace expelled a breath. No, she conceded silently. He was right. She couldn't do that. Not even to avoid an embarrassing interview with Jack.

'Forget it,' she said. 'I just called to say that if I do see Jack, I'll speak to him. But I'm not promising anything, Sean.'

She rang off then, mainly to avoid his gratitude. She didn't want to hear him giving her any credit, when she so felt she didn't deserve it.

Turning back to her mirror, she saw her hair had tumbled down about her shoulders, its red-gold brilliance only accentuating the pallor of her face.

Why had she done it? she wondered. Why had she agreed to speak to Jack? Was it only because she was afraid of what Sean might do without her involvement? Or was she really desperate to prove she didn't care about Jack, either?

Abruptly getting up from the vanity, she opened a drawer and pulled out a black sports bra and matching sweats.

She'd go for a run, she thought. She needed some air; she needed to escape the confines of the pub.

Bundling her hair into a ponytail, she pulled on her canvas trainers and left the room.

Jack was tying the aft rope to the mooring when he looked up and saw a tall slim figure, dressed all in black, pounding along the pier.

It was Grace.

He knew he would have recognised her anywhere. Even without the glorious fall of hair, swinging from side to side with every step she took.

He hadn't realised she liked running. But then, what did he really know about her? Just that she was warm and responsive, that she felt and smelled and tasted delicious. That looking at her, even from a distance, caused him to get an instant hard-on.

And when he was with her...

Dammit!

He didn't want to have this reaction to her.

Just because she had full rounded breasts—with those perky little nipples that had swelled so delightfully against his palms—and slim but curvy thighs, ending in a tight bottom that fitted perfectly into his hands, didn't mean she was unique.

He'd thought Lisa was unique, but Debra had destroyed that image. Okay, he suspected there'd been more malice than compassion in her revelations, but he'd had to accept that her words had aroused some suspicions.

His mother's reaction, when he'd phoned her to ask about Debra's—as he'd thought—jealous claims had clinched it. And, while Siobhan Connolly had done her best to assure him that he shouldn't take anything Debra said seriously, that she was a loose cannon, there'd been something in her voice that had persuaded him she knew more than she'd said.

The call had left him bitter but resigned. He'd thanked God he no longer loved Lisa. Was this why his parents hadn't put up much of a fuss when he'd said he was leaving Kilpheny? Living in the village, there'd always been a chance that someone would say something out of line.

Whatever, he'd noticed that his wife had been significant by her absence since Debra had returned to Ireland. Was that why she'd been hanging around? Had she been waiting for him to find out the truth? He'd decided in the past couple of days that he didn't really care.

Now he climbed the iron ladder to the jetty and called, 'Grace!' before common sense prevented him from doing so.

But what the hell! Sean had been conspicuous by his absence, too, since the money had been transferred to his account. And after what Jack had learned in recent days from his securities expert, he owed the other man no favours, either.

Grace had halted, arrested by the sound of his voice. But then, turning, she put on a spurt and ran back along the pier towards the quay.

Jack blinked. But then, ignoring his conscience, he vaulted over the handrail onto the pier and raced after her. He easily overtook her, despite the length of those gorgeous legs.

'Hey,' he said, catching her arm and feeling an instantaneous connection. He brought her to a standstill and released her. 'Don't I warrant a hello or something?'

Grace swallowed a little convulsively. Here was her chance to speak to him, so why was she drawing back?

In a tight navy tee and baggy black shorts, Jack should have looked nerdy. But he didn't. He looked incredible and she felt all the muscles in her stomach contract.

'I don't know,' she managed now, trying to control her breathing. 'Do you?'

'Why'd you run away?'

Grace shook her head, intensely conscious of the protective limitations of a sports bra. She couldn't prevent her breasts from peaking, could feel the nipples taut against the tight cotton.

'If you hadn't noticed, I'm running,' she said, with what she hoped was a distracting gesture towards her joggers. 'I can't stand around talking. I'm getting cold.'

'So let me show you my boat,' said Jack recklessly, immediately regretting the invitation. Had he lost his mind? If he took her down onto the *Osprey*, he wouldn't be responsible for his actions.

'I don't think so.'

She'd refused him, and Jack knew he should leave

it there. This was the first time he'd seen her since that encounter at Culworth, which was far too prominent in his mind to make any kind of social gesture credible.

'Afraid?' he asked, his brain clearly having no control over his mouth.

'Of course not.' Grace held up her head. 'I just wouldn't want you to put yourself out on my account.'

'I'm not putting myself out,' said Jack drily. 'I really thought you might be interested.'

If she was honest, Grace knew she was interested. But he hadn't been far from the truth when he'd asked if she was afraid.

Now she said quietly, 'I think it would be best if I continued with my run.'

'Why?' Jack wouldn't let it go. 'Despite what you said that night, I get the feeling you resent me for taking advantage of you.' He grimaced. 'Well, believe me, you can't regret what happened any more than I do myself.'

Grace licked her lips. 'I'm sorry.'

'Don't be. These things happen. You're a beautiful woman, Grace. I wanted you. But I guess that goes without saying.'

Grace pursed her lips. 'I expect you've said that to lots of women before,' she offered, trying to lighten the mood, but Jack only grimaced.

'Not as many as you'd think,' he replied with a rueful shrug of his shoulders. 'Come on, Grace.

Can't we be friends?' He paused. 'We could always talk about Sean. How is your boyfriend, anyway? Has he told you how he's spending my money?'

It was a crass thing to say, but Jack couldn't help it. He was doing his best to be friendly, even though it was taking every ounce of self-control he had. When was she going to get the message about Sean? Dared he tell her? But, no, there were some things even he wouldn't do.

Grace stared at him. 'Not exactly,' she said now. Not at all, actually. 'But I imagine he's invested it. In—in starting up the website.'

'Yeah, right.'

Once again, Jack was tempted, but he couldn't tell her that half the money had already gone to paying off debts Sean had probably not told her about. Debts for entertaining, that he suspected weren't business-related. Like hotel rooms that had been occupied by two.

Grace was frowning now. 'Has—has Sean been in touch with you?'

She meant this evening, thinking that would be a load off her shoulders. But then, if Jack had been here on his boat, how could he have spoken to Sean? She doubted Sean had Jack's mobile phone number. Any more than Jack had his.

'I haven't heard a word from him,' replied Jack after a moment. 'Look, forget what I said. Just go and enjoy the rest of your run.' He turned back towards the pier. 'I've got a couple of things to finish off before I go home.'

Grace chewed at her lower lip. Talking about Sean had reminded her what she'd agreed to do. To talk to Jack; to make some excuse for the delay in Sean sending the contract.

To keep Jack sweet!

As if she needed any encouragement, she thought painfully.

Bitterness clogged her throat, but she found herself saying, 'Maybe I would like to see your boat, after all.' She shrugged. 'Can I change my mind? It's a woman's prerogative, isn't it?'

Jack's hands balled into fists, but he forced himself to turn back to her. What could he say? He'd offered the invitation, hadn't he?

'Sure,' he said, ignoring his misgivings. But he couldn't help wondering what had caused this sudden change of heart.

'Okay.'

She wrapped her arms about herself, as if she truly was as cold as she'd claimed earlier.

And Jack's jaw hardened at the thought that he could warm her. Where Grace was concerned, it would be no hardship at all.

Yet he had to keep his head. After all, her sudden change of heart had been unexpected, to say the least. He couldn't help the suspicion that the money he'd given Sean had played a part in it. There was something far too ingenuous about her acquiescence.

But what did that matter? He wanted to spend time with her. He'd take any chance to be with her again.

How the hell was he going to keep his hands off her?

Jack gestured back towards the iron ladder now. 'Can you make it down that thing, or would you rather go round to the steps?'

Grace pulled a face. 'I think I can manage,' she murmured drily.

Then wondered if she'd been entirely wise in her estimate when he went ahead of her to provide a barrier if she fell.

But she didn't miss her footing and Jack didn't touch her, so all was well. She stepped down onto the narrow slip that ran between the rows of craft feeling much warmer than before she'd started.

'It's this way,' he said, going ahead of her again, and, although she'd been expecting a luxury cruiser, the *Osprey* turned out to be a sailing yacht. Some forty feet of polished woodwork and silver-painted hull.

'Oh!'

Grace pressed a hand to her mouth, enchanted by the boat's beauty. Twin masts rose from its gleaming deck, chrome rails adding a touch of elegance.

'D'you like her?'

Jack's tone was surprisingly diffident, and Grace didn't hesitate before giving him an honest reply.

'I love it,' she said, shaking her head in admiration. 'I never expected anything like this.'

Jack's lips tilted. 'I won't ask what you did expect,' he murmured wryly. Then, stepping onto the gunwale, he jumped down onto the deck. 'Give me your hand.'

Grace took his hand without thinking and immediately felt a bolt of electricity shoot up her arm. Jack felt it, too. She was almost sure of it. And she snatched her hand away as soon as her foot touched the planking.

There was a moment when she thought Jack was going to say something. His eyes darkened, and her heart, already pounding in her chest, seemed to rise into her throat.

But the advent of another craft into the marina caused the *Osprey* to rise and fall on the draught.

Unbalanced—physically and mentally—Grace tried to save herself. She groped for the handrail. And, not finding it, suddenly found herself squatting on her bottom on the deck.

It was so unexpected, so unladylike, that she couldn't stop herself from giggling. The tension was released, and Jack, who'd been concerned she might have hurt herself, found a relieved grin spreading over his face.

'I guess you haven't found your sea legs yet,' he said humorously. He held out his hand to help her up. 'We'll have to do something about that.'

Grace didn't want to touch him again, but it would

have been churlish not to. His strong, cool fingers curled about her hand, and the electricity she'd felt before fairly sizzled up her arm.

'Thank you,' she said, releasing herself. Then, before he could say anything more, 'Are you going to show me around?'

CHAPTER THIRTEEN

JACK TOOK A deep breath. He told himself he had no intentions to kiss her. But who was he kidding?

From the moment she'd taken his hand to board the boat, he'd been fighting a battle with himself. He wanted her, dammit. He'd acknowledged that. And he'd provided himself with the ultimate temptation.

But she'd drawn back, and he assured himself he was grateful. And how difficult could it be, showing her round the boat? He was proud of the *Osprey*. It was one of the positive advantages that inheriting his grandmother's money had given him.

Turning, he spread a hand to encompass the whole craft.

Then he said, 'Well, this is it. My home away from home. What do you think?'

'It's not as big as I expected,' admitted Grace, taking her cue from him.

'It's big enough for me,' Jack returned, relaxing a little. He pushed his hands into the front pockets of his shorts.

'There's a main cabin. A master suite. A guest cabin, and the galley, of course. Although I have to say, I don't do much cooking on board.'

Grace smiled and he thought how incredibly attractive she was. 'Do you cook?' she asked half mischievously, and Jack pulled a face.

'I do a mean omelette,' he told her drily. 'And I have been known to produce an edible Bolognese, on occasion.'

Grace glanced about her. 'I'm impressed.'

'Which is a first,' he murmured, and she gave him a sardonic look.

'I'm not so difficult to please,' she assured him, wrapping her arms about herself as the breeze off the marina swirled about them. 'Can we go below?'

'Of course.'

Belatedly Jack took her lack of clothes into consideration. She must be cold. Okay, he admitted, taking her below decks was playing with fire, but what was new?

Expelling a breath he'd hardly been aware he was holding, he gestured towards the companionway. 'Along here,' he said, ignoring the rush of blood that invaded his groin. 'Watch your step.'

A flight of stairs led down to a lower hallway. Jack switched on concealed wall lights as he descended the steps.

Following, Grace sucked in a breath of admiration. Like Lindisfarne House, the yacht was exquisitely designed.

A wide doorway was at the foot of the stairs. Jack had already gone into the main cabin, and Grace hesitated when she reached the entrance.

Comfortable banquettes, bright with cushions in

a variety of colours, lined the walls. Bleached oak woodwork matched the sofas and a thick beige shag carpet covered the floor.

'Come on in.'

Jack was standing between the seating areas. Amazingly, despite his half-disreputable appearance, Grace thought he didn't look out of place. Even the growth of stubble on his jawline only added to his dangerous appeal.

And, in the close confines of the cabin, she could smell his heat, the stark masculine scent of his body.

Forcing herself to concentrate on her surroundings, she crossed the threshold and saw that the galley opened off the other end of the cabin. A breakfast bar provided a useful separation between the two areas, tall chrome-legged stools offering a casual seating arrangement.

She shook her head. 'It's amazing!'

'It's practical,' Jack replied without conceit. But she could tell he was pleased with her reaction. 'Does your father own a boat?'

'No.'

Grace wondered what he would say if she told him her father was having a struggle to make ends meet. After the running expenses of the pub, having to pay a mortgage every month was no joke.

'How about you?' he asked. 'Do you like sailing?'

'I used to think I would,' she confessed ruefully. 'But my dad took me out on one of the fishing boats when I was quite young.' She grimaced.

'After spending most of the trip throwing up, it sort of squashed my enthusiasm.'

'I guess it would.' Jack chuckled, realising how much he enjoyed talking to her. He glanced towards the galley. 'Would you like something to drink?'

She watched as he stepped around the breakfast bar, the baggy shorts hanging precariously from his lean hips. He bent to open the door of what she now saw was a fully equipped fridge and freezer, his tee shirt separating from his shorts, treating her to an appealing wedge of smooth brown skin.

'I've got orange juice or cola,' he said, straightening. 'Or beer.'

And that's not all, thought Grace, taking a breath, and admitting to herself how little her agreement to help Sean had to do with her being here.

'Um—nothing, thanks,' she managed after a moment.

Despite the fact that her throat was dry, she doubted if she could swallow anything right now. She sighed, and then, realising she shouldn't delay any longer, she added, 'I have to tell you, Sean phoned before I came out.'

'Did he?'

Jack closed the fridge door with a definite thud. He wished she'd mentioned that before he'd invited her onto the boat. He didn't want to talk about Sean Nesbitt here.

Turning, he regarded her consideringly. 'So you were planning on meeting me?'

'No.' But Grace couldn't deny she'd been hoping to see him, anyway. 'That is—not exactly.' She shifted uncomfortably. 'As a matter of fact, he said he'd heard from some financial advisor of yours.' She offered a nervous smile. 'He's worried because the website's taking longer to set up than he originally thought.'

Ain't that the truth?

Jack swallowed his annoyance. There was no use blaming Grace for the way Sean had behaved. What irritated him most was that she seemed unaware of his duplicity.

Perhaps she was. He wanted to tell her what her boyfriend was really like, to explode that bubble she seemed to be living in. But he couldn't do it. Not knowing his own motives were anything but impartial.

Jack scowled, turning away again so that she couldn't see his face. But what the hell was he supposed to say? That it didn't matter? That Sean needn't worry? But was he tempted to be generous because he had an ulterior motive?

It seemed he'd got himself into another dangerous situation so far as Grace was concerned.

It certainly put what he'd learned about Lisa into perspective. The feelings he felt when he was with Grace left no room for any other woman—dead or alive—in his life.

'I don't think you have to worry about Sean,' he

said now. Then, unable to stop himself, 'Did he say when he was coming up again?'

Jack was regarding her inquiringly and Grace wrapped her arms about herself once more. 'Um— no,' she admitted awkwardly. 'Did you want to see him?'

'Not particularly.' Jack couldn't prevent that answer. Then, keeping a healthy space between them, 'Why don't you sit down?'

Grace licked her lips and he wondered if she had any idea how provocative that was. 'I should go,' she murmured uneasily. 'I haven't finished my run.'

'Okay.'

With a determination born of self-preservation, Jack moved across the cabin towards the door. If she wanted to go, he wasn't going to stop her. In fact, it was probably the most sensible thing he'd done tonight.

She turned as he would have passed her, and he sensed she was as uneasy as he was. Green eyes met his with undisguised emotion in their depths. And when her lips parted to allow her tongue to escape again, he knew he'd had every reason to be apprehensive.

And let's face it, he thought, she was temptation personified and he'd created this situation himself.

'Dammit, Grace,' he muttered, reaching for her, and she stumbled forward into his arms. 'This was so not meant to happen. It is not why I invited you on board.'

'Isn't it?'

Grace was having her own little crisis of conscience. Not least because she knew she had initiated this, not him.

But for Jack, feeling her lips yielding beneath his was the purest kind of torment. The knot in his belly tightened and a groan vibrated in his chest. God, how much more of this could he take? he wondered. He felt as if he were on the verge of losing his mind.

He couldn't prevent his tongue from seeking the moist cavern of her mouth. Was thrilled when he felt her tongue twine with his tongue and the hungry urgency of her body against his.

She might have been cold before, but she was burning up now.

His leg was wedged between her legs, and he could feel the tremor in her thighs. And knew the urge to lower her onto the soft carpet and strip what few clothes she was wearing from her body.

But some small corner of his brain was still functioning, reminding him that getting involved with her again would be a mistake.

He didn't want to let her go, but he had to. Even if a certain part of his body wasn't with the programme. He had to use his brain, not his sex. He only hoped she wouldn't look down and see the bulge that swelled his shorts.

Grace, meanwhile, had wanted Jack to kiss her. Had wanted more than that, if she was honest. But when Jack drew back and his narrow-eyed gaze raked her face, she knew he was having second thoughts.

'I think we'd better cool it,' he said, a shade harshly. 'Much as I want you, I'm not a complete bastard, whatever you think.'

'Jack...'

'You said you were leaving,' he said, turning aside from her. 'If you want to finish your run, it's getting late. I wouldn't like to think of you out there after dark.'

'Do you care?'

'Of course I care,' he muttered. Then, brushing past her, 'Let's go.'

Grace tucked her hands beneath her arms, aware that her heart was racing. 'Thank you for showing me your boat,' she said, earning a sardonic look from him.

'My pleasure,' he said drily, stepping back to allow her to precede him out of the cabin.

But when he emerged into the small hallway beyond, he almost ran into her. He'd expected her to start up the companionway, but Grace was studying a door at the end of the hall.

'Is—er—is that the loo? I mean—the head?'

Jack looked along the hall and made a negative gesture. 'You need the bathroom?'

Grace's colour deepened. 'My hands are sticky. I'd like to wash them.'

'Hey, you don't have to give me a reason,' said

Jack drily. Even if this was the last thing he'd wanted to do.

He eased past her and led the way along the hall. Beyond the door, a double cabin, its wide bed covered with a bronze silk spread, looked far too inviting.

'The head's through there,' he said, pointing to a door across the cabin. 'Take your time.'

When the bathroom door closed behind her, Jack backed out of the cabin. He could have waited, but he decided she could find her own way up onto the deck.

Mounting the stairs himself, he went to check the mooring lines. He'd already checked them once, but what the hell? he thought. You could never be too careful.

In more ways than one.

However, when a good five minutes had passed and there was no sign of Grace joining him, Jack went to the top of the companionway and looked down.

Where was she?

Then he thought he heard a faint cry.

Without stopping to identify it, Jack ran quickly down the stairs again. He glanced into the main cabin, but there was no one there. After only a moment's hesitation, he strode towards the forward stateroom.

'Jack!'

He could hear Grace's voice now. Clearly. She

was evidently still in the head and he wondered, not without some apprehension, why she would be calling him.

'Yeah?' he said, pausing only briefly before circling the bed to the bathroom door. 'You okay?'

'Would I be shouting for you if I was?' countered Grace from inside, and it was obvious she was seriously miffed. 'I can't get the door open.'

Jack suppressed a laugh. 'Have you tried lifting the lock?'

'What lock?' Grace sounded confused. 'I didn't lock the door when I came in.'

'No, but I guess the lock dropped, anyway,' said Jack patiently. 'It does that sometimes. If you lift that small circular latch and slide the door along—'

The door opened before he'd finished speaking. Grace stood there, her face flushed with embarrassment, and Jack did the unforgivable. He started to laugh.

Grace didn't laugh.

She stared at him with hurt, angry eyes and then attempted to push past him to get out of the cabin.

'Hey…' Jack sobered. 'I'm sorry. But nobody's locked themselves in my head before.'

'And that's hilarious, isn't it?' Grace exclaimed, frustrated by his refusal to get out of her way. 'Did anyone ever tell you how juvenile that kind of humour is?'

Jack sighed. 'Okay, okay. Maybe I was a bit thoughtless—'

'A bit!'

'All right, a lot thoughtless.' Jack gazed down into her humiliated face and knew an emotion that he'd never felt before. 'I'm sorry, sweetheart—'

'I'm not your sweetheart,' she exclaimed, lifting her hands to push at his chest.

But Jack lifted his hands also, capturing hers in his and bringing the knuckle of first one hand, then the other, to his lips.

'I didn't mean to upset you,' he said softly, his breath, warm and slightly scented with coffee, fanning her hot temple. 'Come on, Grace. You know I was only teasing.'

'Do I?'

Her eyes were still mutinous, but Jack knew she was softening towards him.

'Sure you do,' he said huskily. And then, because he was seduced by her indignation of all things, he pulled her closer.

'Jack!'

But her use of his name, whether encouragement or protest, was lost beneath the urgent pressure of his mouth.

Once again, Grace's lips parted, almost without her volition. Jack's mouth was warm and sensuous, his kiss hard and purposeful. In seconds, she was swept with a feeling of heat and need, numbing her to any thought of resistance.

Hot and weak with longing, she felt his tongue press urgently into the moist hollow of her mouth.

It was both a driving assault and an intimate exploration, causing a flood of wetness to make itself felt between her legs.

Her whole body felt consumed by their mutual hunger and a delicious tremor of anticipation caused her to slip her hands about his waist.

Between his tee and the low waistband of his shorts, firm, slightly moist skin spread smoothly beneath her palms. She wanted to push her hands inside his shorts and cup his buttocks, but she wasn't quite that sure of his response.

Nevertheless, when Jack gripped the backs of her thighs, lifting her against the powerful thrust of his erection, she parted her legs eagerly.

She wanted him closer, much closer. Male flesh disappearing into female flesh; brown on white; skin on skin.

She wanted *him*, she thought without remorse. She'd only felt this alive on one other occasion in her life: that morning, on the beach at Culworth.

But what did that make her?

Whatever, she couldn't pretend any longer that she was doing this for Sean.

It was what she wanted, heaven help her! And like an addict, she couldn't get enough of the drug of Jack's lovemaking.

With her nails digging into his hips, she arched against him, telling him without words how vulnerable she was. When his stubble grazed her cheek, she gloried in the sensation, enveloped in a cocoon of sensuality that left her weak and totally lost.

He pushed the sports bra up above her breasts and she shivered in anticipation when his mouth closed on one swollen peak. He nipped at her with his teeth and she trembled violently.

She felt more excited than she'd ever been before.

'Jack,' she choked, clutching at the waistband of his shorts as her legs turned to jelly beneath her. 'God, Jack—please!'

And then the boat rocked as someone came on board.

Grace froze, but Jack apparently retained his mobility. He pulled her sports bra down over her breasts, the nipples still wet and throbbing from his tongue.

'Stay here,' he said in an undertone, leaving her to stride across the cabin.

She heard him walking swiftly along the corridor and then the sound of his feet climbing the stairs.

Envying him his control, Grace took a moment to check her appearance in the mirror in the bathroom. Her hair had come loose from the ponytail she'd secured before leaving the pub and red-gold strands tumbled about her shoulders. Her mouth looked swollen and bare of any gloss.

But she'd been running, she defended herself. No one seeing her now would necessarily suspect what had been going on.

She pulled a face. Who was she kidding? She looked as if she'd just got out of bed.

She wished.

She ran delicate fingers over her mouth as she moved across the cabin. It did feel bruised and tender. She could only hope no one would notice.

She wondered who would come on board without asking permission. It could be anyone. She didn't know any of Jack's friends.

And then she heard her father's voice and froze again.

'Mr Connolly,' he said politely, and she heard Jack make a similar response.

Then Jack added, 'Can I help you?'

There was a moment's silence while the two men seemed to be taking each other's measure.

'Perhaps.' Tom Spencer sounded less confident now. 'I wonder—have you seen my daughter?'

'Grace?'

As if she had a sister, thought Grace ruefully. But then her father didn't know how much Jack knew about her.

'Yes, Grace.' There was a trace of impatience in her father's voice now, and Grace wondered why he would think Jack might know where she was. 'Jim Wales, the harbour master, said he saw you talking to her earlier.'

'Ah, yes...'

Grace didn't know what Jack might have said then. Whether he would have condemned himself further by telling an outright lie, which she couldn't allow.

With a feeling of resignation, she left the cabin and ran along the corridor, mounting the stairs two at a time until she was facing the two men.

'I'm here, Dad,' she said flatly, before Jack could answer him. 'What do you want?'

Tom Spencer looked at Grace, then at Jack, before returning his attention to his daughter again.

'Your mother was worried about you. Are you aware of the time?' he demanded tersely.

Grace wasn't, but she took a surreptitious glance at her watch and saw it was much later than she'd imagined.

'It's half past nine,' she said shortly. 'I didn't know there was a curfew.'

'Grace!'

Her father clearly didn't appreciate having to have this conversation in front of Jack.

'It's late enough for a young woman out alone. Particularly one who's barely half dressed.'

'I've been running, Dad.'

'Have you?' Tom Spencer's eyes turned to Jack again. 'Well, it looks as if Mr Connolly caught you. Or were you both going to pretend you weren't here?'

'I invited Grace to look over the boat, sure. I assumed she was old enough to make her own decisions.'

Tom Spencer's lips tightened. 'Of course she is

old enough,' he said stiffly. 'I just wonder if that was all you had in mind.'

Jack was taken aback by the accusation. As far as he was aware, Grace's parents knew next to nothing about him.

'Dad,' Grace began, between her teeth, but Jack didn't need anyone to fight his battles.

'I'm sorry if by inviting Grace on board I've upset your wife,' he said neutrally. 'Please give her my sincere apologies.'

Tom Spencer straightened his shoulders. Despite being a fairly tall man, he was still several inches shorter than Jack.

'I'll do that, of course,' he said, even though Jack was sure it pained him to say it. He paused. 'I wonder, has your other female visitor left?'

It was Jack's turn to look confused now. 'My other female visitor?' he echoed. 'I'm not sure I—'

'The lady George Lewis picked up from the airport,' Grace's father said with some satisfaction. 'I believe she told him she was staying with you for a few weeks.'

Jack stifled an oath.

Grace was looking completely stunned by this revelation, and Jack wanted to hit the other man for ruining what had been one of the best—no, *the best*—night of his life.

'Yes. She's gone,' he said, not attempting to avoid the question.

He tried to catch Grace's eye, but she wouldn't look at him, so he continued on regardless.

'Debra Carrick—the young lady you mentioned—is my sister-in-law.'

'Your sister-in-law?'

Grace was looking at him now, but once again her father destroyed the moment.

'You knew Mr Connolly had been married, Grace,' he said, turning to her. 'I'm sure Sean mentioned it to you.'

Jack knew the use of her boyfriend's name had been deliberate, but Tom Spencer wasn't finished yet.

'It's good to know you have people who care about you, Mr Connolly. People who can share your grief at the tragic loss of your wife.'

CHAPTER FOURTEEN

JACK WAS IN a foul mood when he got back to his house.

He couldn't believe what had happened; couldn't believe how strong a desire he'd had to shove his fist down Grace's father's throat.

The man was a complete moron, he thought bitterly. He'd behaved as if Grace were Little Red Riding Hood and Jack were the Big Bad Wolf. Dammit, Spencer knew nothing about him, and that crack about Lisa had been below the belt.

Of course, Grace had left with her father. She'd had little choice when he'd said he'd brought his car. Despite what Jack had said, she probably had her own suspicions about Debra. And who could blame her, with her father looking on as if he'd achieved a coup?

Besides, she was still Sean's girlfriend. Another fact her father had felt the need to emphasise.

Which made the way Jack was feeling now somewhat less than princely. He'd never gone after another man's woman in his life. He ought to be ashamed, not finding reasons to blame her father. He could imagine what Tom Spencer would say if he ever found out the truth.

Yet, in spite of all the obstacles, there was something about Grace that made him act in a way he hardly recognised. He felt an inexplicable mixture of tenderness and lust towards her, feelings that defied any explanation he could give.

And tonight, he'd been fairly sure she felt the same connection, a connection that her father had tried his best to destroy.

Well, Jack had to accept that nothing was going to come of it at present. However Grace felt, she couldn't have mistaken Jack's antipathy towards her father.

He'd been a fool, he thought. He should have cooled it. Right now he felt that if he walked into the Bay Horse, Tom Spencer would have him thrown out.

Of course, good old Sean might turn up this weekend, but Jack wasn't holding his breath. He might even produce the contract he'd originally agreed to provide, but, after Grace's comments, he doubted that was on the cards.

It was a reason he could use to talk to Grace again, but was he really that desperate to regain her trust?

He suspected he was. He suspected he was only kidding himself if he thought this might pass.

Going into the kitchen, he switched on the light and found Lisa sitting on the breakfast bar.

It gave him quite a start. And after tonight's fiasco, he was in no mood to speak to her.

'What's wrong? Did someone rain on your parade?' she said, without her usual air of confidence.

'Apart from you, you mean?' asked Jack sharply, and she pulled a face. 'Oh, yeah, I got the low-down from your sister. No wonder you've never talked about the crash.'

Lisa made a dismissive gesture. 'I told you before, Debs is in love with you. She'd say anything if she thought it would make you notice her.'

Jack had been running water into the coffee pot, but now he turned to regard her with narrowed eyes. 'So it's not true?' he said. 'You weren't having an affair?'

Lisa sighed. 'I was in love with you, Jack, re-member? We were good together, weren't we? Why would I need anyone else?'

Jack shook his head and turned off the tap. 'You tell me,' he said, switching the coffee pot on.

But the truth was he didn't care any more. And how depressing was that?

'I was a good wife,' Lisa protested. 'Your house was always clean. You got your meals on time.'

'Yeah, thanks to Mrs Reilly,' said Jack drily. 'I don't recall you doing much about the house.'

'I didn't have to.' Lisa was indignant. 'But that doesn't mean I was unfaithful.' Lisa stretched out a hand to consider her nails. 'And if that's what you're all twisted out of shape about—'

'It's not.'

'Really?' Lisa sounded almost disappointed. Then, staring at him, she said, 'It's that girl, isn't it?

The one who came here with Sean.' Her laughter tinkled suddenly. 'Oh, how ironic is that!'

Jack scowled. 'What do you mean?'

But he was too late. Lisa had gone, fading into the darkness as if she'd never been there at all.

He must be going out of his head, Jack thought wearily, aware of a disturbing sense of unease.

But, as he carried his coffee out of the room, he thought he could still hear Lisa's laughter echoing in the quiet house.

Grace worked in the pub on Saturday night.

She hadn't wanted to, but Rosie Phillips had apparently taken another trip to Newcastle. And Grace's mother simply wasn't up to serving behind the bar.

She'd assured herself that if Jack came in, she'd treat him like any other customer. After all, she'd managed to do that before. And although she knew her father had only been trying to cause trouble by bringing up Jack's sister-in-law's visit, all he'd really done was remind her that Jack still loved his late wife.

But she needn't have worried. The bar was busy, but Jack wasn't amongst the customers.

Consequently, by the time she went up to bed, she wasn't feeling very happy.

It was a week since she'd seen Jack; a week since she'd reluctantly accompanied her father off his boat. And while common sense told her she'd be wise to forget all about him, she wasn't having a lot of luck.

She couldn't help thinking about what had happened, couldn't help acknowledging that if her father hadn't interrupted them they'd have ended up in Jack's bed. In that beautiful cabin, she reflected ruefully. She ought to be grateful things hadn't got that far.

Only she wasn't.

In addition, there was an uncomfortable truce between her and her father. He hadn't asked her why she'd been on Jack's boat and she hadn't volunteered her reasons for being there.

In truth, she hardly knew what those reasons were any more. Why had she agreed to his invitation? She'd known the dangers, known how reckless she was being. But somehow when she was with Jack, she forgot everything else.

Grace shed her clothes, feeling utterly depressed. As she stepped into the shower she wondered when her life was likely to return to normal. She seemed to spend her days lurching from one disaster to another.

The water was hot, but Grace ran it as cool as she could bear it. Her whole body felt hot, and, when she soaped her breasts, she felt how aroused she was.

Sean had never made her feel like this, she conceded, soaping the rest of her body. She sighed. How pathetic she was, needing another man in her life.

She slept fitfully, only falling into a deep slumber towards morning. In consequence, it was after eleven o'clock when she opened her eyes.

Something had awakened her, she thought, pushing herself up on her elbows. Then she blinked when the door across the room opened, and her mother's face appeared.

It was unusual to see her mother up so early. Susan Spencer had lost so much weight during her illness that she was only a shadow of her former self.

'Ah, you're awake at last,' she said, pleased to see her daughter was sitting up. She came into the room and closed the door. 'You've got a visitor. Sean's here.'

'Sean?'

For a moment, Grace had hoped it was Jack.

And how pathetic was that?

Besides, Susan Spencer had never met Jack. And she had no doubt picked up on the fact that her husband wasn't enthusiastic about Grace seeing another man.

Now, however, Grace didn't let any of this show in her face. Since her mum had been ill, there was no question of upsetting her.

'Yes,' said her mother now, bending to pick up the underwear her daughter had discarded the night before. She viewed the scraps of cotton and lace with some bemusement. 'I don't know how you wear these things, Grace. They can't be very warm.'

'They're not supposed to be,' said Grace drily, flopping back against her pillows.

The realisation that Sean was downstairs, probably chatting with her father, filled her with misgivings. What was he doing here? Had he expected her to get in touch with him after she'd presumably spoken to Jack? Was that why he'd decided to make the journey himself? Or was he hoping to persuade her that his relationship with Natalie West wasn't serious?

'Anyway, it's time you were up,' her mother went on, tucking the dirty clothes into the basket in the bathroom. 'It's not like you to spend so long in bed.'

'I didn't sleep well.' Grace raised an arm to cover her eyes. 'When did Sean get here?'

'About fifteen minutes ago,' replied her mother. She still looked a little frail and Grace felt guilty at her making the effort to tidy her room. 'I'll tell him you're coming, shall I? I know he's impatient to see you.'

'But I'm not impatient to see him,' muttered Grace barely audibly, but this time her mother heard her.

She paused. 'Why not?'

Grace groaned. 'It's a long story, Mum.' She was loath to upset her. 'He's not the man you and Dad think he is.'

Mrs Spencer frowned. 'Well, I must admit I wasn't very keen when he persuaded your father to invest in his business.' She hesitated. 'But you know what your father's like. And I know he's hoping that the business is a success. We could all do with some extra cash, couldn't we?'

Grace groaned. 'Oh, Mum…'

'You won't be long, will you?' Her mother moved towards the door, evidently not wanting to hear any more. 'I believe Sean's driven up from London this morning and he's planning on driving back this evening. He looks tired, Grace. Perhaps he's come to give us all some good news. We could certainly do with it, couldn't we?'

'Why?' Grace gazed at her mother anxiously. 'You're not—you're not—'

'Ill again? No.' To Grace's relief, her mother shook her head. 'But I know your father's worried about the pub's finances. He could do with not having to pay that mortgage every month.'

'Oh, Mum…'

Grace shook her head. Of course her father was worried. And it was all her fault. Somehow she had to get Sean to spend some of the money Jack had given him to help her father out.

'I'll have a shower,' she said now as her mother opened the door. 'I won't be long.'

Her mum's smile deepened. 'Oh, good. I'll tell him.'

You can tell him I resent him coming here, preying on my parents, thought Grace bitterly.

But this time she spoke beneath her breath.

By the time Grace went downstairs, it was after twelve.

Apart from having a shower, she'd washed her hair as well, and it had taken a little time to blow-dry.

Then she'd dressed in pleated shorts and a candy-pink halter, high-heeled wedged sandals completing her outfit.

Sean was outside, sitting at a table in the beer garden, enjoying a pint of lager. He was on his own but had apparently struck up a conversation with a couple of girls sitting at a table nearby.

From her position in the doorway, Grace could see there was a lot of giggling going on, and she guessed Sean was exercising his doubtful charms.

Then he saw her and got immediately to his feet.

'Hey, beautiful,' he said, and Grace wanted to die of embarrassment when this caused more giggling from the other table.

She went reluctantly towards him, but when he would have touched her, she kept firmly out of his reach.

Undaunted, Sean grinned. 'You look stunning,' he said, as if she cared what he thought about her.

'Why are you here?' Grace countered shortly. 'Have you come to pay your debts?'

Sean grimaced. 'Don't be like that.' He glanced behind him. 'At least sit down with me. Have a drink.'

Because she didn't want to cause a scene in front of the other girls—and her parents—Grace subsided onto the bench beside the table.

'I don't want a drink,' she said flatly and then had to wait with grim impatience while Sean summoned the youth who helped out at weekends and ordered himself another beer.

'What's going on?' she continued, after she'd regained his attention. 'Do I take it you've been in touch with Jack?'

'Hell, no.' Sean scowled. 'And what do you mean by hanging up on me the other night? I don't like it when people hang up on me and then turn their damn phones off.'

'Well, tough.' Grace wasn't worried about offending him. 'What's happening about the website, or am I not supposed to ask?'

Sean hunched his shoulders. 'I'm getting there,' he muttered. 'I'm getting there.'

'Doing what, precisely?'

Sean glared at her. 'Hey, I don't have to answer to you.'

'Don't you?' Grace arched her brows. 'Don't you think my parents deserve an explanation? And you do have to answer to Jack. From what you've said, he sounds pretty peeved.'

Sean's eyes narrowed. 'Did you go to see him?'

Grace hesitated. 'I've seen him,' she admitted reluctantly. 'I met him when I was out running the other evening. He was working on his boat and he saw me when I ran along the pier.'

'Clever.' Sean regarded her expectantly. 'So I guess you saw his boat, too? What's it like? Some big expensive motor yacht, I'll bet.'

'It's not that big.' Grace was equally reluctant to

discuss the boat with him. 'It's not a motor yacht, either. It has sails.'

Sean pulled a face. 'Typical. Jack would go for something that needed a bit of skill to handle it. Lisa always used to say he never took the easy way out.'

'You knew Lisa?' Grace was intrigued in spite of herself. 'You never said.'

'Well, of course I knew her.' Sean's second beer arrived and he took a generous swig before continuing, 'Lisa was a good kid. She—well, she and I had some laughs together.'

Grace didn't know why, but Sean's words troubled her. There'd been a note of arrogance in his voice when he'd spoken of Jack's late wife. Almost as if he knew something that Jack didn't.

'Anyway,' he went on, 'what happened when you saw Jack? What did he say?'

'What did you expect him to say?' Grace was impatient.

'You told him what I was worried about?'

'I'm not a child, Sean. But I got the impression he didn't want to talk about it to me.'

Sean groaned. 'So you didn't try a little…womanly persuasion?'

'No!'

But Grace's colour deepened at the duplicity of her reply.

However, Sean put an entirely different interpretation on her embarrassment. 'I should have known better,' he muttered. 'You always were a cold fish. I bet even a guy like Jack, with all his advantages, would have his work cut out trying to get you into bed.'

Grace was stunned. And hurt.

She wanted to say Sean couldn't be more wrong. That she wasn't cold at all. That Jack was twice the man he was, in more ways than one. But she couldn't do it.

She wouldn't give Sean that kind of ammunition to use against the other man, whatever the provocation. Instead, she schooled her expression and pushed herself to her feet.

'Get lost, Sean,' she said succinctly. 'And don't come back until you can pay Dad what you owe him.'

'Hey, I don't owe your old man anything,' retorted Sean staunchly. 'He chose to invest in the website. If it hasn't worked out, that's not my problem.'

'You're not serious!'

'Of course I'm serious. People invest in stocks and shares all the time and get shafted. He can't come crying to me because his investment hasn't worked out.'

'You bastard!'

Grace got up from the table, her face suffused with angry colour. Sean rose, too, obviously furious that she'd insulted him within the hearing of the other girls.

'Jack's said something, hasn't he?' he demanded.

His mouth compressed into a thin line. 'He's been blabbing about where the money's gone.'

'Jack's said nothing about the money,' said Grace contemptuously. 'But if he knows you as well as I do, I'm surprised he lent you any money in the first place.'

'I bet he has.' Sean wasn't listening to her. 'I should have known he'd take any opportunity to put me down. Lisa always said—'

He broke off at that point and although Grace wanted to leave, she felt frozen to the spot. What on earth had Sean been about to say?

'He doesn't understand what it's like for me.' As if regretting his last words, Sean seemed eager to change the subject. 'I've never had any money to splash around.'

Grace groaned. She could hardly believe now that she'd felt sorry for him when he'd lost his job. Or that she'd ended up paying his debts for him while he was out of work. The salary she'd earned at the CPS hadn't been huge, but she'd been happy to contribute to their expenses. Which, in all honesty, was why she had so little money now.

But then she'd discovered he didn't own the apartment they were living in. The money she'd given him to help him out with the mortgage had gone into his pocket. He'd even been behind on the rent.

What a fool she'd been.

Then she'd lost her job, due to cutbacks, just after she'd found him with Natalie. In a way, it had come at exactly the right time. She hadn't needed an excuse to leave, but one had been provided for her. If her parents hadn't been involved, she'd never have seen him again.

But they were involved and she'd been stupid enough to think that, whatever he felt about her, he wouldn't let them down.

'Look, if you want to see Jack, I suggest you go and see him,' she said wearily. 'Tell him you're having problems. He might agree to help you out.'

'You think?' Sean's scowl deepened. 'So—you'll come with me, right?'

'You're joking!'

'No, I'm not.' Sean regarded her derisively. 'If you don't want me to go into the pub and tell your old man he's not getting his money back, you'll do everything you can to keep me sweet.'

CHAPTER FIFTEEN

JACK WAS IN the study he'd furnished for himself on the first floor of Lindisfarne House when he heard the doorbell.

He'd been engrossed in his study of his plans for the cottages, and trying not to think about Grace. He had decided to knock down the walls dividing the kitchen and living rooms to create a through room, which was both lighter and more contemporary in design.

But the interruption meant he had to abandon the work and go and see who was at the door. The only person he really wanted to see was Grace herself, but he didn't think there was much chance of that.

Then he had an unpleasant thought.

It was Sunday. How could he have forgotten? Sean came to visit his girlfriend at weekends. Bearing in mind what Jack had learned Sean had done with at least a part of the money he'd loaned him, it was possible Sean had decided to come clean about his debts.

His pulse quickened in spite of himself.

What if Grace was with him? He had wanted to see her again, but not with Sean.

Nevertheless, the knowledge served to weaken the bitterness he felt towards the other man. However badly Sean had behaved, his own behaviour beat that hands down.

He had a brief hope that it wasn't Sean. He could see no sign of the Mercedes on his drive through the glass panels in the door.

But when he opened the door, he saw the reason for his error. The car was parked at his gate and Sean was already halfway down the path towards it.

But he heard the door opening and turned, his expression a mixture of disappointment and resignation.

'Hey, Jack,' he said, retracing his steps with evident reluctance. 'I was beginning to think you weren't home.' He grinned. 'Long time no see.'

'Yeah.'

Jack was no more enthusiastic for this meeting than his visitor. And despite his reluctance to see Grace in the other man's company, it was obvious Sean was alone.

'Can I come in?'

'Sure. Why not?' Jack stepped back from the door. Then, because he couldn't help himself, 'Isn't Grace with you today?'

'Uh…no.' Sean shrugged his shoulders indifferently as he passed Jack. 'She's back at the pub. Helping her mum and dad.'

'She didn't want to come?'

Jack knew he shouldn't persist, but he couldn't help himself.

'I guess not.' Sean walked into the living room

and flopped down on a leather sofa. Then, shouldering off his jacket, 'That's better. And cooler. Do you have air conditioning or what?'

'No. No air conditioning,' said Jack evenly. 'The walls are thick. They keep the inside of the house cool.'

'And warm in the winter, I'll bet.' Sean nodded sagely. 'There's a lot to be said for old buildings. Present company excepted, of course, but some of these new developers don't have any idea.'

Jack made a non-committal movement of his head and regarded the other man expectantly.

'I agree,' he said. 'But I doubt you came to see me to discuss modern architecture.'

He paused, pushing his hands into the back pockets of his jeans and rocking back inquiringly.

'I imagine you've got some news for me about the website.'

Sean's face reddened. 'It's getting there,' he said evasively. 'I've had a few problems to contend with, actually.'

'Like what?'

Sean was bitter. 'I know you've been checking up on me. You always were a close-fisted bastard!'

Jack's eyes widened. 'I don't think it's unreasonable to show some interest in my investment,' he said mildly. 'I wouldn't be much of a businessman if I handed over one hundred thousand pounds without expecting some feedback.'

'I told you at the time you gave me the money

that I'd keep you informed of what was going on,' exclaimed Sean resentfully.

'But you haven't, have you?'

'What do you mean?'

'Correct me if I'm wrong, but it has been over six weeks since we spoke last.'

'Yeah, but I've been busy. Ask Grace, if you don't believe me. This is the first time I've been up to Rothburn since that weekend we came here. And I only arrived this morning, so you can't accuse me of avoiding you, can you?'

Jack frowned.

'I thought you came up every weekend.'

'Is that what Grace told you?' Sean sounded pleased. 'She doesn't like it when I neglect her.'

Jack's nails dug into his palms. 'She'd hardly tell me, would she? It's nothing to do with me.'

'No.' Sean conceded the point. 'But it's not easy, trying to juggle two careers at once. If I'd had more time, I'd have got more done.'

Jack's gaze grew guarded. 'You've had six weeks,' he pointed out, and Sean pulled a face.

'With shift work and a dodgy manager,' he muttered gloomily. 'You try finding inspiration in those circumstances.'

Not to mention Sean's trip to Las Vegas, thought Jack scornfully. Had he spent all his free time in bars and casinos? Just where did Grace figure in that scenario?

'Anyway…' Sean looked up at him. 'If it's an apology you want, you've got it. I haven't been the most reliable of partners, I admit it.' He pulled a wry face. 'I'll try to do better in the future.'

'Right.' Jack conceded the point. 'So tell me, have you found other investors?'

'Other investors?' Sean was suspicious. 'Why would you ask a question like that?'

'It's a reasonable question.' Jack spoke evenly. 'I'm wondering how much money we're dealing with here.'

Sean scowled. 'What has Grace told you?'

'Grace?' Jack's expression was guarded. 'Grace hasn't told me a thing.'

Sean's eyes narrowed. 'So—okay,' he said. 'There are no other investors. It's not that easy to find spare money in the present climate.' He glanced about him. 'Well, how about offering me a beer, Jack? I'm driving back to London tonight and I'm thirsty.'

'You're not staying over?'

'Hell, no. I've got to be back at work first thing Monday morning.'

Jack despised himself for his own reaction to this news. Was it possible Grace hadn't slept with Sean since that first weekend?

'Of course, I'd certainly have more time to work on the website if I was like you,' he continued, apparently unaware that Jack's demeanour had changed. 'I've said it before and I'll say it again, it must be nice to be a millionaire.'

Jack held Sean's gaze for a long minute. Was this

the overture to another demand for money? The guy couldn't be serious, he thought. He couldn't possibly think Jack would send good money after bad.

'Hey, I meant to ask you…'

Jack had stepped into the hall to get Sean a beer— as that was all he was likely to get—when the guy's voice called him back.

And Jack prepared himself for the inevitable request.

But that wasn't it.

'I understand you saw Grace the other evening, when she was out running,' he remarked casually.

Jack stiffened. 'Yeah, I did,' he admitted, wondering where in hell Sean was going with this.

'I gather you showed her over your boat,' Sean went on, his gaze speculative. 'You and she seem to get along together pretty well.'

Jack shrugged. 'She's a nice girl,' he said tightly, inwardly wincing at his lack of honesty.

But Sean's next words drove every other thought out of his head.

'You know, I wouldn't mind if you wanted to take her out sometime,' he said casually. 'She's lost touch with most of her friends here and I guess you could do with some female company yourself.'

Jack's jaw dropped. 'You're not serious!'

Sean's chin jutted. 'Why not? Don't look at me like that, Jack. It was only an idea.'

'A bad idea,' said Jack harshly, turning back into

the hall. His teeth ground together for a moment.
'I'll get your beer.'

'Hey, don't be such a puritan, Jack.' Sean got up
from the sofa and came after him. He paused in the
doorway, supporting himself with a hand on either
side of the frame. 'You like her, don't you? And it's
not as if we've never done such a thing before.'

Jack stared at him blankly. 'I don't know what the
hell you're talking about,' he muttered.

''Course you do,' declared the other man blandly.
'I mean, when we were at college in Dublin, we used
to switch girlfriends all the time.'

'Did we? I don't remember that.'

Jack gripped the frame of the door until his
knuckles whitened. Despite Sean's facile response,
Jack had the feeling that there was more to this than
met the eye.

Was this about Grace, or was it about Lisa? Jack
knew, with a feeling of resignation, he couldn't be
absolutely sure.

He was grateful when Sean didn't follow him into
the kitchen but turned back into the living room. He
didn't think he could be civil to the man right now.

Whatever way he looked at it, it seemed that Sean
was bargaining with his girlfriend. Was Jack supposed to compensate Sean—financially, of course—
for the privilege of screwing Grace?

God, what a situation!

He knew he could never treat Grace that way. In

truth, in all this awful mess, she was the only shining light.

He flung open the fridge door, scowling at its contents. Could he honestly drink beer with the other man without giving in to the disgust he was feeling and throwing him out?

His own part in the affair might fill him with loathing, but Sean's behaviour almost compensated for it.

Of course, Jack had never cheated on his wife. But then, he'd never known what temptation was until he'd met Grace.

Thinking of Grace in this context made him feel sick. Pulling out a bottle of beer—he was sure if he tried to drink anything, it would choke him—he tried to control his scattered emotions.

And to cap it all, he couldn't help wondering if Grace had known what Sean was planning to say.

He knew if he wanted to retain any self-respect, he'd stay out of both Grace's and Sean's way in future. She might be innocent of any deception, but for his own sanity's sake he couldn't take that risk.

Sean was standing by the window when he returned to the living room.

'Great view,' he said, accepting the beer Jack handed to him. 'You're a lucky man, Jack. But then, you've heard me say that before.'

Jack frowned. 'Yeah,' he said tightly. 'It was at my wedding, wasn't it? You were complimenting me on finding Lisa. Telling me what a lucky man I was.'

Sean shrugged. 'Well, you were—you *are*,' he amended, flinging himself onto the sofa again. 'You can't deny it, can you?'

'As you are?' suggested Jack, hooking a hip over the arm of the chair opposite. 'What about Grace?'

Jack didn't know what was driving him, but he was heartily sick of trying to humour the other man.

'Grace?' Sean stared at him. 'I don't know what you're talking about.'

'Well, she's a beautiful woman. You're supposed to care about her, aren't you? I'd say that makes you a lucky man.'

'Yeah, yeah.' Sean snorted. 'What are you getting at, Jack? I haven't said any different, have I?'

'You've virtually offered me the chance of sleeping with her,' retorted Jack harshly. 'My God, I'd never offer a woman I loved in exchange for cold, hard cash!'

'You didn't have to.'

The words were barely audible, but Jack had excellent hearing.

'What did you say?' he demanded, getting to his feet, and Sean had the grace to lower his head.

'Nothing. I said nothing,' he muttered in an undertone. 'Forget it. You obviously don't fancy Grace. I don't blame you, actually. She can be a cold fish at times.'

'I want to know what you meant,' Jack persisted, crossing the floor and hauling the other man to his feet. 'Come on, Sean. What are you saying? This isn't about Grace, is it? It's about Lisa!'

'I don't know what you mean.'

'I think you do. I spoke to Debra recently and she made some very interesting comments.'

'Debra!' Sean scoffed. 'Surely you don't believe a word she says. She's been in love with you for years. She'd say anything to get your attention.'

'I don't think so.' Jack stared into the other man's eyes. 'Why don't you tell the truth for once? Or is that too much to expect?'

Sean scowled. 'Don't tell me you never suspected.'

'Suspected? Suspected what?' Jack controlled the desire to get physical with an effort. 'Are you saying you were having an affair with Lisa?'

'As if you didn't know.' Jack's restraint was giving Sean more confidence. 'Yes, I had sex with her, Jack. Lots of times, as it happens. She was bored with you, man. All you could talk about was work—'

His voice was strangled by the grip Jack suddenly had on his collar. Dragging Sean up in front of him, he got seriously in his face.

'You know,' he said almost thoughtfully, 'Debra said as much, but I wouldn't believe her. What about the night she died? Were you with her then?'

Sean struggled to get some air, but it was a losing battle. 'I—I might have been,' he got out through a choked windpipe. 'So what? I didn't cause the crash.'

'She was taking you home, though, wasn't she?'

Jack realised that that was where Lisa had been going. She'd sworn to him that evening that she wasn't going out, which was why her death had been such a terrible shock.

'Maybe.'

Sean was evidently weighing his options. The odds of telling Jack the truth against the unlikely event of being able to lie his way out of it.

The truth won out, because he suddenly cried, 'She was mad about me, Jack. You can't blame me because I did what any red-blooded man would do.'

Jack could, and he would. But gauging the satisfaction he'd get out of flooring the other guy, against the story Sean would no doubt make up to account for his injuries to Grace and her family, changed his mind.

With a muffled oath, he opened his hands and let Sean stumble away from him.

'She must have been desperate,' he said flatly.

And the amazing thing was he honestly didn't care.

Recovering a little, Sean tugged at his collar. 'She was crazy, too.' He took several shuddering breaths. 'She drove like a maniac, you know. I thought I was done for when that petrol tanker turned the corner!'

Jack was about to say he didn't care whether the other man had suffered because of the accident or not when Sean's expression abruptly changed. His attempts to defend himself were silenced by the look of absolute horror that crossed his face.

He was looking beyond Jack, towards the doorway into the hall, and, judging by the contortion of his flushed features, Jack suspected they were no longer alone.

He was guessing Grace had decided to join them after all, though he hadn't heard her enter the house. But the room behind him was empty and there seemed no reason for Sean's behaviour, for the unmistakeable terror in his gaze.

Sean blinked several times, his mouth opening and shutting as if he wanted to say something, but couldn't quite get the words past his trembling lips.

Then, almost hysterically, he said, 'What the hell is that?' He swallowed convulsively. 'How— No! No, this isn't happening.' He shook his head as if by doing so he could deny what he was seeing. 'I know what you're trying to do to me. You want me to think I'm going out of my mind.'

And then Jack knew.

He didn't need to hear Lisa's voice or see her slender form wavering in the doorway. Sean's reaction was answer enough. His late wife had chosen to show herself to someone else as well as him.

And although he knew he shouldn't, he couldn't prevent himself from saying innocently, 'What are you talking about, Sean? As far as I'm concerned, our conversation is over. I never want to see your miserable face again.'

'But—Jack—'

Clearly Sean needed some reassurance, but Jack

didn't see why he should comfort someone who had abandoned Lisa when she needed him most.

'Just go,' he said, and Jack guessed Lisa hadn't made it easy for him when Sean practically fell over the coffee table in his haste to get out of the room.

Jack was still standing, hands balled at his sides, when Lisa said wistfully, 'You're never going to forgive me now, are you?'

Jack shook his head. 'I forgave you a long time ago, Lisa,' he said ruefully. 'I just hope Grace understands.'

CHAPTER SIXTEEN

GRACE HAD HAD a particularly tiring day at the agency and she was looking forward to getting home and taking a nice long bath. It hadn't helped that William Grafton had turned up again, asking about a property in Rothburn. He said he'd heard she was looking for an apartment and he was planning on turning an old house on Rothbury Road into three separate units.

As if she'd want to live in some apartment he owned, thought Grace with a shiver. She'd never feel safe from his intrusion, no matter how many locks she had on the door.

She only hoped her father wouldn't hear of it. Knowing that he liked the man would make her position very difficult if that was so. And her heart sank when she arrived home that afternoon, and Tom Spencer asked if he could have a word with her.

He and Grace's mother were having a cup of tea in their living room. The family quarters were at the back of the pub, away from the public rooms and kitchen.

Grace's anxiety lessoned a little when she saw that Susan Spencer looked positively radiant. Surely her mother wouldn't be so pleased if she thought Grace was leaving and getting her own place?

'Would you like some tea, Grace?' she asked, when her daughter came into the room. 'Your father's just made it.'

'No, that's okay, Mum.' Grace wasn't really in the mood for chit-chat. Then a wonderful thought struck her. 'Have you had the all-clear from the hospital?'

'Not yet.' Mrs Spencer pulled a wry face. 'But soon, I hope.' She looked up at her husband, who was hovering in the doorway. 'Do come in and sit down, Tom.' Then, to her daughter, 'We've got some good news for you.'

It was the proposed apartment, thought Grace miserably.

Oh, God, how was she going to get out of this?

'Do you mind if I go and get changed first?' she asked, trying to sound positive. 'It's been a long day.'

'Well, this won't take long,' said Mrs Spencer. 'Tom, why don't you spit it out? I have the feeling Grace won't be half as disappointed as you think.'

Disappointed?

Grace frowned. 'Is something wrong?'

'Well, from our point of view, something's very right,' said her mother shortly. 'Tom, for heaven's sake, be grateful that you haven't lost all that money. All right, you haven't made any money, either, but, from my point of view, that's a blessing.'

Grace blinked. 'What money are we talking about?' she asked, hardly daring to believe what her brain was telling her.

'The money I lent that no-good boyfriend of

yours,' said her father, shocking her anew. 'Apparently he's had a change of heart. He's not going ahead with the website.' He paused, glancing significantly at his wife, and then added ruefully, 'I hear he's leaving the country and trying his luck in the States.'

Grace's jaw dropped. 'Are you saying you've got your investment back?'

'Every penny of it,' agreed her mother proudly. 'I told your father that I didn't think you'd be too broken-hearted, but he thinks you'll blame him for not kicking up more of a fuss.'

'A fuss about what?'

'Well, you're in love with the man, aren't you?' her father demanded. 'Why do you think I got the money for him in the first place?'

'Oh, Tom, don't blame Grace.' Mrs Spencer regarded her husband with some resignation. 'You know you could see yourself as a company director. Not to mention the fortune you thought you were going to make.'

Grace's father looked a little shamefaced. 'Anything I did, I did for all of us,' he protested, and his wife gave him a reassuring smile.

'I know, Tom. You're a star,' she said mischievously.

'But I can't say I'm sorry Grace isn't going to marry Sean.'

Grace was shocked and stunned. And hardly able to believe it.

'You mean, you'll be able to pay off the mortgage?' she asked weakly. And when her mother nodded, 'Oh, thank goodness. I was so afraid you'd never get your money back.'

'I was afraid of that, too,' confessed her mother honestly. 'So you're not heartbroken at Sean's change of heart?'

Jack entered the bar of the Bay Horse, not without a trace of apprehension.

It was a week since Sean had left and Jack was sure now he wouldn't be coming back.

Sean had driven away from Lindisfarne House ten days ago as if the devil himself were at his heels. Or perhaps a she-devil, Jack decided drily, remembering how he'd felt when Lisa had first appeared to him.

Now, however, Jack had decided to take control of his life and speak to Grace. She might not want to speak to him. He could easily have misread the signals she'd been giving him. But learning about the Spencers' involvement had certainly given him hope.

When he'd asked Sean whether there were any other investors, he'd already known that Grace's father was heavily involved.

Despite his conceit, Sean knew little about business, and he'd had no idea his financial dealings would be so easy to expose. When Jack had first given him the one hundred thousand, the firm of advisors who worked for him in London had immediately investigated the viability of Sean's proposal. That was how Jack had learned how Sean was spending the money; including the trip to Las Vegas and the fact that Sean hadn't been alone.

Jack was praying that, while there were no guarantees that the fact that her parents had been involved explained her reasons for staying with Sean, now that he'd returned her father's money, she was not committed any more.

Or was he only clutching at straws?

He'd chosen a time when he thought the pub might not be crowded. Even visitors staying overnight tended to be gone by afternoon. And it was a nice day; ideal for the beach. He should have been at Culworth himself.

Pushing open the door into the bar, Jack paused to get his bearings. As he'd expected, the place wasn't busy, only a couple of regulars shooting balls around the pool table.

And Tom Spencer polishing glasses behind the bar.

Great!

Jack had hoped to avoid Grace's father. He had no desire to have another argument with the man. But he was here and—oh, joy!—he'd seen him. Jack allowed the door to swing closed behind him and moved across the floor.

'Hi,' he said pleasantly, laying a folded jacket on the counter. He paused, and when the other man didn't say anything, he went on, 'Sean left this at my house a couple of weekends ago. Perhaps you'd give it to him the next time he's here.'

Tom Spencer put down the glass he was polishing and folded his arms. 'Nesbitt won't be coming here again,' he said flatly. 'But I can ask Grace to send it on to him, if you like.'

'Okay,' Jack said, with a shrug of his shoulders. 'That'd be good. Thanks.'

He was turning away, deciding he'd try to speak to Grace some other time, when Tom Spencer spoke again. 'May I offer you a drink, Mr Connolly?' he asked civilly. 'I feel I owe you an apology. I was somewhat less than courteous the last time we met.'

To say Jack was taken aback would have been an understatement. The last thing he'd expected from Grace's father was civility. He'd been fairly sure the man didn't like him, and getting cosy with him now seemed slightly hypocritical somehow.

But he was Grace's father, and time and events had certainly blunted his dislike of the man. So he said, with equal courtesy, 'Thanks. I'll have a bottle of beer.'

Tom Spencer nodded and bent to take a German lager from the chilled cabinet. Then he set the beer and a glass on the counter, levering off the cap with professional ease.

'Do you mind if I join you, Mr Connolly?'

Jack managed not to show his surprise. 'Please,'

he said, and the other man drew himself a half of bitter from the tap.

There was silence for a few moments while they both swallowed a mouthful of beer. Jack didn't use the glass, but drank his straight from the bottle.

Then Tom Spencer spoke again.

'Grace won't be seeing Nesbitt again,' he remarked evenly, wiping foam from his upper lip with the back of his hand. He paused, eyeing Jack closely. 'Did you know?'

Jack wanted to say, *How could I?* But this wasn't the time for provocative questions.

So he said, 'No,' with what he hoped was just the right amount of interest. 'I haven't seen Sean since he left my house over a week ago.'

Tom Spencer frowned. 'His choice or yours?'

Jack didn't want to answer that. 'Does it matter?'

The other man sniffed. 'But you're not sorry they've split up?'

'No.' Jack decided to tell the truth. 'Are you?'

'Me?' Spencer grimaced. 'Hell, no. I've known for some time that he wasn't to be trusted.' He paused. 'But I thought Grace loved him. That was why I acted the heavy father that night on the yacht.'

Jack was taken aback. 'Well...' He was surprised at the man's honesty. 'I don't know what to say.'

'You could tell me if I'm wrong in thinking you want Grace for yourself,' Spencer remarked drily. 'If you don't, then I can only thank you for what you've done for Susan and me.'

Jack caught his breath. 'I beg your pardon…'

'I'm not a fool, Mr Connolly. I know I behaved foolishly in lending Sean all that money, but, believe me, I've paid for my mistake. These past few months have been tough, for all of us. The Bay Horse makes us a living, but, you must know, pubs aren't as popular as they were.'

Jack stared at him. 'I still don't…'

'I'm fairly sure you gave Sean the money to pay us back,' said Grace's father quietly. 'I've not told anyone, but I heard him talking to Grace when he was here that weekend. He as good as told her he'd lost my money, that I wouldn't be getting it back.'

'I see.'

'He wanted her to go with him to see you, but she refused. He said he'd tell her mother and me what was going on, but for once she didn't give in to his threats.'

He paused. 'He never came back. I couldn't understand it, but Grace said he had to get back to London.'

Jack nodded. 'I guess he did.'

Tom Spencer frowned. 'What did you say to him, Mr Connolly? Did you tell him you knew where all the money had gone?'

'I don't remember,' said Jack, taking a mouthful of his beer. 'But I'm glad things have worked out well for you. I wouldn't have liked to see you lose this place.'

'Nor would I, Mr Connolly. Nor would I.' He hesitated.

'But I warn you. I'm not going to allow you or anyone else to hurt my daughter again.'

'Dad!'

The shocked exclamation startled both men.

Jack looked beyond her father's determined stance to where Grace was standing in the doorway to the private quarters beyond.

'Dad, what on earth do you think you're doing?' she demanded. 'Accusing Jack of hurting me!' She swallowed, avoiding Jack's eyes and the look of condemnation she was sure she would see in them. 'He didn't. He—he wouldn't. Don't judge all men by Sean's standards.'

Jack tried to catch her eye, but she wouldn't look at him. And before he could say anything, Tom Spencer turned to speak to his daughter.

'What are you doing home, Grace?' he asked in surprise. 'It's barely half past three.'

'I had a viewing near here and Mr Hughes gave me the rest of the afternoon off.'

She made a helpless gesture. 'It's just as well he did. What have you been saying to Jack behind my back?'

Her father gave Jack an appealing look. 'We've been having a civil conversation, Grace. That's all.'

'I brought Sean's jacket,' Jack broke in. 'He left it at the house. And I don't have his address.'

Grace looked at him then, her beautiful green eyes

dark and cloudy. She'd apparently worn a pantsuit to work today, and the slim-fitting trousers emphasised the sexy length of her legs.

'Well—I'm sorry,' she said, shifting a little nervously beneath his disturbing gaze. 'My father had no right to speak to you as he did.'

Her father sighed then. 'You weren't supposed to hear this conversation, Grace. And I have no intention of apologising for speaking my mind.'

He paused, casting another glance in Jack's direction. 'Mr Connolly hasn't had to listen to you crying yourself to sleep every night for over a week now—'

'Dad!'

Grace wanted to die of embarrassment, but her father wasn't finished yet.

'You can't deny it, Grace. We've heard you, your mother and me. And I have to say, we've been worried sick.'

Grace closed her eyes for a moment. And then, holding on to the door frame for support, she said tightly, 'My—my crying myself to sleep has nothing to do with...with Jack.'

'I know.' The older man evidently surprised her with his words. 'But I hope to God you haven't been crying yourself to sleep because Nesbitt has apparently dumped you. I thought you had more sense than that.'

Grace didn't know where to look. Jack was staring at her, she knew it. She could feel those intent dark eyes searching her face.

Oh, God, she thought, what must he be thinking? That the humiliation she was suffering was well-deserved.

'He didn't.' Grace's lips trembled. 'If—if you must know, I dumped him weeks ago.'

Jack felt an incredible sense of relief. Dear God, he did have a chance, after all.

'Well, thank heaven for that!'

Jack's statement came out of nowhere, and Grace rubbed her hands along her forearms under the sleeves of her jacket, feeling the nervous chill in spite of the heat of the day.

Her eyes widened. What was he saying? Had he come here to see her? Dared she believe such a thing?

She was struggling for words, when Jack continued, 'Surely you realised I would want to know?'

Grace's tongue circled her upper lip. 'Why—why would I think that? We haven't even spoken to one another since that night you showed me…your boat.'

And that was such an understatement. But she could hardly say, the night you almost seduced me in the cabin. Not in front of her father.

'Well, I wasn't sure you'd want me to get in touch with you,' exclaimed Jack drily. 'You must have known I'd want to see you again.'

Grace lifted her shoulders. 'You didn't try very hard to stop me from leaving with Dad.'

'Because I thought you were still involved with

Sean.' He sighed, giving her father a rueful look. 'I felt bad enough as it was, knowing how I felt.'

'How did you feel?' she asked a little breathlessly, and at last Mr Spencer realised this conversation wasn't for him.

'I'm going to get a couple of crates up from the cellar,' he said, earning Jack's gratitude. 'If you'd like to stay for supper, you're welcome.'

As soon as he'd gone, Jack groaned. 'You know how I feel about you,' he said savagely. 'Dammit, Grace, I haven't exactly kept it a secret, have I?'

Grace looked at him uncertainly. 'Do you think we should continue this conversation up in my room?'

Jack regarded her narrowly. 'I thought you'd never ask.' He moved quickly along the bar and she lifted the hatch to allow him to step through.

A dog-leg staircase led up to the first floor. Grace went ahead, shedding her jacket onto the banister, revealing a simple vest of coral-pink silk.

The colour should have clashed with her hair, but somehow it didn't. And Jack had to resist the urge to slip his hand beneath its hem and find the soft skin of her midriff.

Her bedroom wasn't big, but it was attractive. Pale walls were complemented by floral curtains and a matching bedspread, a taupe carpet underfoot soft beneath their feet.

Grace was nervous. As she kicked off her heels, going ahead of Jack into the room, she was half expecting a continuation of the awkward exchange they'd had downstairs.

But Jack merely leaned back against the door to close it and then reached for her. He pulled her against him with urgent hands, sliding long, possessive fingers into her hair.

'Sweet,' he said, a little hoarsely, and bent his head.

His mouth nudged hers, took possession of hers, her lips parting to allow the hungry access of his tongue. He licked his way along her lips, causing tremors of delight to consume her, so that when his tongue plunged into her mouth, she heard herself moan with pleasure.

His eyes were open, searching her face for confirmation that she wanted him. She lifted her hand and stroked his jawline, loving the incipient stubble of his beard. She could hardly believe that Jack was here, in her bedroom. She'd despaired of ever being with him again.

Jack knew he had to take this easy, but it was incredibly difficult when what he really wanted to do was tumble her onto her bed. But she deserved to know how he felt about her. For him to hear how she felt about him.

Yet the temptation to just go on holding her and kissing her, feeling her slender body yielding—oh, so deliciously—against his, was almost irresistible.

He had missed her so much. God, even in his best moments he hadn't been able to kill the fear that, despite what they'd shared, she'd forgive Sean and marry him.

Losing her, he knew, would have been so much worse than losing Lisa. He'd loved his wife, of course he had, but it had been such a shallow thing compared to his love for Grace.

He caught his breath.

When had he first realised he loved her? he wondered. At the cottages, when she'd practically fallen into his arms? Or that afternoon on the beach, when he'd made love with her, uncaring that anyone might have seen them?

Or had it been on his yacht, when her father had interrupted them so inopportunely? All of the above, he suspected. He couldn't remember a time since he'd met her that he hadn't felt this amazing connection between them.

He released her mouth to bury his face in the curve below her jawline. Her skin was so smooth, so soft, and the heat of her body came to him in waves. That and the unmistakeable scent of her arousal, an arousal he felt his body mimicking when she lifted one leg and wrapped it around his calf.

'Do you want me?' she breathed, and Jack felt his senses reeling.

'Will the sun rise tomorrow?' he demanded thickly as his hands sought the provocative swell of her butt.

'But we need to talk, Grace,' he muttered, his breathing accelerating. 'Besides, I don't know if your father would approve if I made love to his daughter here.'

'Well, he seemed pretty happy about your being here earlier,' she murmured. 'I thought he was angry with you, but he wasn't, was he?'

'No.' Jack smiled. 'I think your dad and I have come to an understanding. He's not such an ogre when you get to know him.'

'Dad's okay,' said Grace, rising up on her toes to press herself even closer. 'I didn't tell you before because I didn't want you to think I wanted you to bail them out, but Dad had mortgaged the pub to help Sean.'

She paused. 'When Sean was here that weekend, he told me Dad wouldn't be getting his money back, that he'd spent his investment. I was horrified. He threatened to tell Mum and Dad if I didn't help him out.'

'Did he?' Jack wished he'd beaten the guy up while he'd had the chance.

'But I wouldn't do it. And believe it or not, Dad got his money back this week.' She sighed. 'You don't know how relieved I was when I heard what had happened. Sean must have had a change of heart.'

'So it would seem,' said Jack neutrally, thinking he had definitely got the best of the bargain, anyway.

Grace wound her arms around his waist. 'You know, I never thought I'd say such a thing, but I'm actually grateful to Sean.'

Jack's brows descended. 'Sean?' he echoed, and her cheeks dimpled at the darkening expression on his face.

'Leaving his jacket at your house,' Grace reminded him, using her free hand to tug his shirt free of his waistband. Her fingers spread against hot, slightly moist flesh, and she rubbed herself against him. 'Hmm, it's hot in here. Wouldn't you like to get out of this shirt?'

There was nothing Jack would have liked more. His pants, too, he thought ruefully. There was no doubt that they were getting much too tight.

'Grace—love, I want to be sure you know what you're doing here,' he groaned as her fingers slipped inside the waistband of his jeans. His pulse rate went into overdrive. 'I guess Sean didn't tell you what happened when he came to see me?'

Grace closed her eyes for a moment. Then she heaved a sigh.

'How could he? I haven't seen Sean since that afternoon when he went to your house.'

Jack knew this already from her father, but he wanted to be certain. 'He didn't come back to the pub?'

'Well, he wouldn't, would he?' Grace conceded the point. She blew out a breath. 'Okay, perhaps I should tell you that I finished with Sean months ago.' She flushed. 'I found out he was seeing someone else behind my back.'

Jack stared at her. 'But I thought—'

'Yes, I know what you thought,' Grace confessed unhappily. 'But if Sean had thought I was seeing someone else, Dad would never have got his money back.' She gave him a sly look. 'Besides, I'd sworn I wasn't going to get involved with anyone else and you were...well, too much of a temptation.'

Jack caught his breath. 'You're kidding me!'

'No, I'm not.'

'So when Sean came to ask for that loan, and you came with him, it wasn't me you were mad at?'

'No.' Grace sucked in a breath. 'I'm sorry. You must have thought I was a real bitch.'

'That isn't the expression I'd have used,' he remarked wryly, and she gave a little laugh.

Jack shook his head. 'But I have to say I had a few sleepless nights fretting about the way I'd treated Sean.'

'Oh, Jack...'

'It's true.' He gazed down into her anxious face, his own expression softer than she'd ever seen it. 'I was falling in love with his woman, see? I was even thinking of selling Lindisfarne House and moving away.'

Grace shook her head. 'And I thought I was just a diversion. Something to make you forget your grief at losing your wife.'

'Oh, no.' Jack was very sure. 'There's nothing diversionary about my feelings for you, sweetheart. I don't think I've ever felt so desperate as when I thought you loved someone else.'

'You're sure about that?'

Jack's thigh wedged between her legs and he felt her heat in the muscles that drew him in. Her eyes sought his, eyes so green he felt he could drown in them.

'What do you think?' he said as she gazed up at him. 'I just know I've never felt like this before.'

Her lips parted, innocently inviting the invasion of his tongue. She touched his lips with tremulous fingers. 'I love you, Jack. I think I knew it from the moment we first met. Even when I told myself you weren't interested in me, I couldn't deny my feelings. Not to myself.'

'So why didn't you tell me?' he demanded huskily, feeling the rapid tattoo of her heart beating against his chest. 'I've been through hell since you left me on the yacht.'

'Me, too.' Grace pursed her lips. Then, rather tentatively, 'Was that girl my father spoke about really your former sister-in-law?'

'Debra? Oh, yeah.'

Jack caught her chin between his fingers and bestowed a teasing kiss on the corner of her mouth. He grinned. 'She's been my constant defender ever since Lisa died.'

'Does she love you?'

'So I'm told.' Jack didn't specify his informant. 'But as far as I'm concerned, she's Lisa's little sister. A bit of a nuisance sometimes, but she has my best interests at heart.'

Without her input, would he really have connected all the dots about Lisa and Sean?

Grace considered this. 'My father said she must care about you a lot to come here.'

'I guess she does,' said Jack ruefully. 'But you'll like when you get to know her.'

'You think?' asked Grace doubtfully. 'I'm going to find it very hard to like someone who loves you. Unless it's your family, of course.'

'I know the feeling,' he said, lowering his head again to nibble at the side of her neck. 'But at least your dad has decided I'm really not such a bad guy. I'm looking forward to him meeting my ma and pa.'

Grace sucked in a breath. 'Meeting your...your ma and pa?' she echoed confusedly. 'Are your parents coming to stay with you?'

'Well, they may do, in the future,' agreed Jack. 'But I was thinking about before the wedding. Perhaps your mother and father might like a trip to Ireland instead.'

Grace's lips parted. 'Is—is that a proposal?'

'Oh, no.' Jack regarded her mischievously. 'I wouldn't be as presumptuous as that.'

'Presumptuous?'

'Of course.' Jack grinned again. 'I haven't got your father's permission yet, have I? But I will get it,' he assured her. 'Even if I have to get down on my knees.'

'Oh, Jack, I do love you.'

'I hope so.' Jack's voice was a little hoarse now,

and she could feel the throbbing heat of his arousal against her hip. 'So maybe I'd better go down and tell your father how we feel.'

'In a little while.'

Grace was in no hurry. She looped her arms about his neck and threaded her fingers into his thick dark hair. She loved the feel of his body against hers, the sensual scent of male she associated with him. And the intimacy between them that she'd never shared with anyone else.

'I think, you know,' she said huskily, 'we have other business to attend to first.'

EPILOGUE

GRACE HAD NEVER attended an awards ceremony before, let alone one where she'd been asked to be the guest presenter.

And particularly not one where said guest presenter was in the final trimester of her first pregnancy and feeling like an elephant besides.

'I can't do this,' she moaned, gripping Jack's hand so tightly her nails were in danger of puncturing his flesh. 'I've never done anything like this before.'

'There's always a first time,' murmured Jack, his eyes dancing as he looked at her. 'I'm here and I'm your husband. How difficult can it be?'

'But it's the baby,' Grace protested, and Jack grinned at her words.

'Our baby,' he agreed, with some satisfaction. And ignoring the interested stares of their audience, he leant towards his wife and brushed his lips against hers.

Immediately, Grace felt a surge of emotion. Jack only had to touch her and her body melted with his heat. She badly wanted to touch him, too, but they were on stage in front of more than a hundred people. So she contented herself with squeezing his thigh and hearing his indrawn breath.

'Later,' he said in an undertone, and Grace dimpled.

'Is that a threat?' she whispered teasingly, and Jack gave her a smouldering look.

'It's a promise,' he said hoarsely, removing her hand from his leg as the mayor began to speak.

Grace's attention was definitely fractured, however. Even the baby seemed ominously quiet at present. It was probably a silent protest at the way she'd provoked its father, she reflected. Nonetheless, she was so proud of Jack, so proud of the man she had married.

Her hand traced the prominent mound of her belly almost absently. Just a couple of weeks to go, she thought. She couldn't wait for the baby to be here. The sexy jersey crepe was tight across her abdomen, and she'd wanted to wear something less revealing. But Jack had assured her that he'd be the envy of every man there.

At least the dress was warm. Northumberland in March wasn't the warmest time of year. But at least they were in a warm hall and not out on the cliffs at Culworth. They might have been if her father had had his way.

Jack's renovation of the cottages at Culworth was the reason for this presentation. They'd already won an award for originality of design, and Jack had also received a grant from the government to continue renovating other properties in the area.

Consequently, this ceremony had been arranged by the local Chamber of Commerce. They'd decided to honour Jack and in so doing advertise the attractions of the town, as well.

Asking Grace to present the cut-glass set square had, she suspected, been her father's suggestion.

Since Grace and Jack had got married seven months ago, Tom Spencer and Jack's father had become the best of friends. They shared an interest in fishing, and in Irish whiskey. And Patrick Connolly and Jack's mother were in the audience at present. They were frequent visitors to Rothburn these days, much to everyone's delight.

Then it was her turn to speak and Jack squeezed her hand in encouragement as she got up to make the presentation. She had to say a few words first, which was easy. She loved talking about her husband to anyone.

But the formality of the occasion was what had unnerved her. And only when the ornamental instrument was in Jack's hands did she heave a deep sigh of relief.

Then caught her breath as a stabbing pain pierced her abdomen. It almost caused her to double up, but she managed to keep a smile plastered to her face.

However, Jack, always sensitive to her feelings, saw at once that she was hurting. Cutting short his response, he slipped a protective arm about her waist.

'What's wrong?'

Grace looked up at him, her expression a mixture of irony and regret.

'I think it's the baby,' she said. 'They told me at

the clinic that it might come early.' She braced a hand against the lower part of her spine. 'I hate to break up the party, darling, but I think you ought to go and get the car.'

Jack's face mirrored his consternation. 'God, I'm sorry, love. I never should have insisted that you did this.'

'Well, at least you got your award,' murmured Grace, laughing a little breathlessly. 'But right now, I'd like for you to take me home.'

The silence that had first greeted Grace's obvious discomfort was suddenly broken.

Half a dozen sets of footsteps thudded across the stage, among them those of Grace's mother and Siobhan Connolly.

'She needs to go to the hospital,' declared Mrs Spencer, trying to take control. But Grace clung to Jack's hands insistently, not letting anyone else come between them.

'Home,' she said imploringly, her eyes on his. 'Darling, you promised I could have this baby at home.' She took another breath as a second pain ripped through her. 'I'm all right, really I am. Just get in touch with Nurse Forrester and I'll be fine.'

Jack gazed round at his mother and his mother-in-law, hearing their worried protests, and then gave a determined nod.

'Home it is,' he said, ignoring the other women's complaints. 'If you two want to do something useful, offer our apologies to the mayor and his cronies, will you?'

'But, Jack—'

They left the hall with not just the women's protests ringing in their ears, but their husbands', too.

And Jack hoped and prayed he was making the right decision. If anything happened to Grace, his life would be over. He'd realised that a long time ago, and it was never more relevant than at present.

The next few hours were chaotic.

They arrived back at Lindisfarne House to find that Mrs Spencer had contacted Mrs Honeyman and that she had already prepared their bedroom in readiness for the new arrival.

But Grace hadn't wanted to spend the next few hours in the bedroom. She'd insisted on staying with Jack while Mrs Honeyman made them both a strong, sweet cup of tea. In the normal way, Jack would have gagged at the unaccustomed sweetness, but right then everything had taken second place to his concern.

Eventually—and seamlessly—their son was born in the bedroom. Jack had insisted on carrying his wife upstairs as soon as the nurse declared the baby's head was beginning to show.

And John Thomas Patrick Connolly delighted his parents by filling his lungs as soon as Nurse Forrester had delivered him. His lusty cries brought his grandparents to the bedroom, but the nurse wouldn't allow them through the door.

'Give the parents a few minutes,' she said, emerging with flushed cheeks and a smile of satisfaction on her face.

And both the Spencers and the Connollys had to be content with her assessment, forced to kick their heels in the living room while Mrs Honeyman provided them with more tea.

Meanwhile, Jack and Grace were admiring their new baby, whose cries had abated somewhat since he'd discovered his mother's breast.

A mirror image of his father, thought Grace ruefully, aware that Jack was watching his son with awe.

'I told you,' Grace said softly, stroking her husband's cheek with loving fingers. 'I'm tougher than I look.'

'Don't I know it?' Jack pulled a wry face. 'You've always been able to wind me round your little finger.'

'I love you,' Grace said now, reaching up to kiss him, and Jack returned the caress with enthusiasm.

'Love you, too,' he said fervently. 'I've never been happier in my life.'

And he wondered if that was why he'd seen Lisa only the once since she'd scared the bejesus out of Sean.

She'd appeared for the last time the evening after Tom Spencer had told them he'd heard from Sean.

Jack had been sitting at his desk, trying to concentrate on his latest design for a science museum, when he'd become conscious of her presence.

'You're happy,' Lisa had said, a certain wistfulness in her expression. 'Oh, and by the way, you won't be troubled by Sean again. I've taken care of that.'

And apparently she had. The last they'd heard, Sean was emigrating to Australia, and Jack couldn't help wondering if Sean realised that wasn't an escape.

Well, wherever Lisa was, he hoped she'd found her own nirvana at last.

Despite everything that had happened, he'd like to think so.

Now he bent to lift his baby son into his arms. The dark eyes, so like his own, gazed back at him in sleepy contentment.

'He's beautiful,' he said proudly. 'You're beautiful. How did I ever find a girl like you?'

'Just lucky, I guess,' said Grace, her eyes twinkling, and Jack thought how wonderful it was to think they could face the future without any of the ghosts of the past.

* * * * *

*If you enjoyed this story, check out
these other great reads from Anne Mather*

*A WILD SURRENDER
HIS FORBIDDEN PASSION
THE BRAZILIAN MILLIONAIRE'S LOVE-CHILD
MENDEZ'S MISTRESS
BEDDED FOR THE ITALIAN'S PLEASURE*

Available now!

LARGER-PRINT BOOKS!
GET 2 FREE LARGER-PRINT NOVELS PLUS
2 FREE GIFTS!

HARLEQUIN®

Romance

From the Heart, For the Heart